BUT MAMA I LOVE HIM
QUINIECE NOBLE

BUT MAMA I LOVE HIM

QUINIECE NOBLE

I'JALE™
PUBLISHING CO.

First Printing: 2019

ISBN 978-0-578-22870-9

www.ijalepublishing.com

Forward

I have known Quiniece Noble for 12 plus years now. We first met at F.W. Gregory Jr. High School in New Orleans, LA.
We established a long friendship.
Hurricane Katrina hit New Orleans and we had to relocate to different cities which caused us to lose contact. We connected through social media.
One day, I reached out to Quiniece for advice. I quickly noticed that she was a hard-worker, business minded, and genuine person. I was thrilled! With no hesitation we become close from our daily conservations. We grow our friendship.
One thing I love about Quiniece is that she is what she calls an open book.
When she asked me to write this foreword, I felt inspired and agreed as soon as she text me, lol.
Quiniece has shared many trials and tribulations with me. I was surprised because she always remains positive and motivated to do more and better. Plus, I love urban literature ...you all are in for treat!

-Jamesha Stevenson

Dedication

This book is dedicated to my grandmother, who always took me to the library after school.
My mom, who inspires me no matter what.... your hard work and dedication will never go unnoticed.
My family, who always have my back through whatever. My friends, who always cheering me on!
Thanks, I couldn't have done it without all of you!

About the Author

Quiniece Noble is a New Orleans native born and raised.
Quiniece fell in love with books since a child thanks to her grand-
mother who made reading fun.
She is the oldest daughter and grandchild. Mother of one hand-
some son, whom she loves dearly.
After graduating high school, Quiniece decided to study Early
Childhood Education. Ms. Noble earned her Childhood Development
Associate Credential.
She has a passion for children, educating and mentoring. She
wants individuals from urban communities, especially New Orleans to
know that despite their circumstances they can overcome anything!

INTRODUCTION:

But Mama I Love Him is a fiction book, also inspired by some circumstances that happened in real life.

TABLE OF CONTENTS

BUT MAMA I LOVE HIM

Chapter 1: IT'S LITTY: KEKE JONES

"Cash Money Records taking over for the '99 & the 2000 –," The song started.

"Aww shit now!" I ran to the dancefloor before Juvenile's voice could even fill up the nightclub. Though that song was damn near pushing twenty years old now, it could still take the lamest party to turnt, especially right in the same city that song was produced many years ago.

"You know Keke gon' cut up every single time," I could hear my best friend screaming near me while I bounced my ass, completely letting loose. Listen, I needed this night to unwind. Today was a special day. Well, it should have been a special day, but it brought back so many unwanted memories. Every time around this year, the City of New Orleans would get together to celebrate the city's recovery after a devastating hurricane Katrina. So many things and lives were displaced back in 2005. In fact, I don't even want to speak on that. I grabbed the chill shot that was sitting on the table of our VIP section. I knocked it back, wanting to forget the old life I had to leave behind. Before a single tear could fall down my face, someone stood before me. Matter of fact it was a face I hadn't seen in a long time. I wasn't even sure if I wanted to see this face.

"Keke, is that you?" Wazzam Sweetie"
Rolling my eyes, I said, "Nah, it's Tee Tee. I mean who else is this supposed to be?"
"I guess they were right."
"Who is they?" I cocked my neck with so much attitude being released.

"Come on now, Keke. You haven't changed and neither have I. The only thing that changed was our location. You remember who I was when I went in and I'm still the same nigga now that I'm out. I

3

don't have to be in the streets to know what's going on in the streets. You feel me?"

As much as I wanted to pretend like I didn't feel him, I knew better. Standing before me was a blast from the past. Well, I'm not even sure if I could call him a blast. He was definitely from my past and a part of my past that I wanted to forget. Unbeknownst to him, I would never be able to forget him. Maybe because of the way he made me feel and the things he made me do.

"Dollar, you do not need to have people out here checking for me. Okay? I'm good!" I tried to walk off until I felt his strong arms pulling me back.

Damn! How did this nigga get even finer…in the damn pen of all places? How was that even possible? I asked myself. There were three things you couldn't take away from Dollar Tate. The nigga was fine, paid and a real street nigga at heart. Unfortunately for me, I loved all that about him even if it came with some wild ass consequences. Although it had been years since our tumultuous relationship ended, I still tried to find bits and pieces of Dollar in every man I dated after him.

"Who are you walking away from? Do you not remember who I am?" He asked, not smiling one bit.

"Still holding on to that street credit you had many years ago, huh?" I asked sarcastically, trying to step away again. This time, he tightened his grip on my arms. He didn't have to utter a word. The look on his face told me to pipe the hell down. I swear Dollar had that effect on everyone. He could make everyone bow the fuck down. Though I would never tell him, I was also keeping tabs on him while he was in the pen. I'm not going to lie, it made me feel good knowing that he was also keeping tabs on me. I knew there was a chance that I would run into him tonight, so that's why I made sure I put extra effort into what I was wearing and the way I looked. A bitch had to be on fleeced ya heard me! My childhood friend who I found on IG was having a special going. Get a sew in and make up free with lashes.

You know I had to let Rich Hair Queen slay me. Since I was already standing before my past, it only made sense to tell how Dollar and I almost became New Orleans power couple. Fuck a Beyonce and Jay-Z. Have you ever heard of the hood version of Bonnie and Clyde? We even had matching rings We We're GOALS ya heard me Well, that was us!

"Yo, Dollar! I see wazzam with you still got that nasty ass attitude after all this time," someone from behind him interjected. "I think it's time to put her lil' ass back in her place. Kidnap her ass and make her family miss her. She seems to have forgot who she was talking to."

Since Dollar was taller than me, I couldn't see over him until I stretched my legs as far as they could go in the heels. That's when I was able to get a glimpse of who was behind him. It was Mon, one of Dollar 's right hand mans. It's crazy how they were still friends now, after all this time.

Dollar sucked his teeth. "Mon, shut the hell up! I keep telling you that your ass is too bossy when it comes to every chick but that crazy ass bitch you got back at home. You better be just as eager to bust down on a nigga when the opportunity presents itself. I got this under control. Keke just showing out for this lil' audience. I don't pay you to give out commands, I pay you to follow mine. Now go get that mic from DJ ass. I'm tired of Keke tryna shake her ass out here to this bounce music anyway."

"Nigga, you lost the privilege to tell me what I can and can't do when your dumb ass got locked up!" After I said what I had to say, I spun on my heels and attempted to walk away. I needed to get away from Dollar because this hate that I was forcing was only wanting to show that I still loved this man. I didn't get too far before I felt myself being pulled back by him.

"Where you think you going, Ke?" Dollar had the nerve to ask me. He really required an answer as if I was still his bitch. Nah!
Before I could clapback with a sassy response, Jazzy, my best friend intervened.

"Come on now, Dollar. We just came out here to have a good time tonight. We wanted to leave the bullshit and drama back home. Ya know? You know my best friend don't mean any harm."

He looked from her then back to me. "Best friend, huh? You really out here still claiming that? Yo' best friend don't have any fucking manners. Your best friend is out here treating me like I'm some regular guy. Like I'm some pizza delivery type of guy or some basic ass shit. She clearly forgot that I was the same dude that she used to be proud to announce she was fucking with a few years ago. A nigga got locked up and she really thought they threw away the key on me. Now I'm back in these streets and now she's acting like I'm some clown. Right now, I am not fucking with it. It's my damn day too! I worked too damn hard to rise in the ranks of these New Orleans streets. Tell your best friend she needs to give me a sincere apology or her ass won't be leaving this club tonight," he threatened.

Jazzy faced me with the most serious look on her face and then said, "Keke, now you know! If you plan on leaving and going back home tonight, then I suggest you apologize to Dollar. I don't have time to be explaining to your boo why you didn't make it back home tonight."

"Oh, you gotta boo?" Dollar laughed again, but it was a rather dismissive kind of laugh. "Yeah, Keke! Do what your best friend told you to do, otherwise your boo gon' be running down to the precinct to file a missing person report. You may be hard to find, but you know I won't be." That smirk on his face told me that he hadn't changed one bit. He could still get with the shits if need be.

"Really, Jazzy? Was that even necessary to tell him of all people? And besides, I'm not apologizing to his cocky ass. The only person I should apologize to is myself for allowing myself to entertain his cocky ass all over again. Now, are you done turning up? If so, we can go home because I'm no longer in the mood to celebrate," I pouted, upset at Jazzy for putting my business out there. I didn't even want that kind of information disclosed to someone like Dollar of all people.

"Listen, I know you're upset and all but it's just now turning 12:30 according to my phone. And from what I've always known, this club doors don't close until 2 A.M. Feel me," was all she said.

"And? What's that supposed to mean? I'm the designated driver as of tonight," I had to remind her.

"Designated driver? You might as well hand Jazzy your keys now because I'm telling you, you won't be leaving this club until you tell me what I want to hear, Ke," Dollar interrupted our conversation.

"I just can't see you giving out these kinds of commands in prison. Let's keep that same energy, sir."

Suddenly, his entourage broke into laughter as if I had told a funny joke. I heard one of the guys say, "Girl, you just don't know."

"Oh, so let me guess! You just got out too?" Jazzy snickered beside me and discreetly hit my leg. I knew my mouth was too smart for my own good. Truth be told, I couldn't help it. I wasn't always this way, but I had no other choice but to become this way. At the time, Dollar couldn't stand a weak ass female! In order to fuck with a boss, you either had to be one or you had to learn to become one. I bossed the fuck up and now, I couldn't control my tongue.

Dollar nodded his head in the direction of the DJ. And just like that, Mon scurried to the other end of the club to get the mic. Though Dollar's Entourage was still around, I felt myself relax a bit. From the looks of it, he was still hanging with the same people that he used to hang with back in the day. There were about two people that I didn't recognize which shocked me because Dollar liked to keep his circle tight, and he would hardly let anyone in. One thing for sure is that I knew his team was really solid. These guys would literally take a bullet and a charge for him without him even asking them to. That's how solid they were, or I guess I can say that's how dumb they were. It seems like I was the only one inside of Dollar's camp that woke the fuck up once I learned that the Feds were on to him. As much as I loved being known throughout the city as his down ass bitch, I knew that I wasn't ready for everything that came with a kind of lifestyle. I could help him package and sell, but I couldn't take a charge! I think that's what ultimately led to our downfall in our relationship.

I quietly watched as Mon walked back over and handed the microphone to Dollar. Despite Dollar embarrassing him not even a good ten minutes ago, Mon still held his head up high as he walked back over to us. I don't see how he could do that as a man himself, but I respected him for that. The respect that Dollar got only made you respect him, whether you liked him or hated him. You still had to respect him.

As soon as the mic touched Dollar 's hand, I swear the music stopped out of nowhere.

"Aye, thanks everybody for coming out and helping us celebrate yet another holiday in the black community plus my release day. I mean y'all don't have to go home and shit, but y'all have to get the fuck out of here. Right the fuck now! Aye security open those doors and I expect everyone to follow," he demanded then he looked over at me. "Everybody can go home...except you."

The blaring of the fire alarm caused me to semi-panic for a bit and Dollar snatched me up out of nowhere as everyone exited the club in a complete frenzy. I don't know why, but I felt myself relaxing in his embrace that was short lived. I don't even think a full two minutes had gone by before the club was empty of all patrons except the DJ and his crew, the bartenders, and Dollar 's entourage.

"I can't believe you just ended a special celebration almost two hours early to try to prove a point," I called him out, getting fed up with his cocky ass attitude. You would have thought that all that federal time would have at least humbled him a bit but nah. He was just as cocky as before.

Dollar hit me with the infamous Kanye shrug. "Come on now Keke! Out of everyone in here, you know me better than all of them do. I said the party was over and guess what? I see that it worked. Everyone is getting in their whips to go home except you. Just like I thought!"

"Welcome home bastard," I mumbled underneath my breath.

***

CHAPTER 2:
DOLLAR TATE
TRENDING TOPIC

I swear Keke was pissed the fuck off at me, but it didn't faze me one bit. Truth be told, her attitude had always been fucked up after getting heavily involved with me. It wasn't always like that. I must give Keke some credit though. Though she was sitting up here pouting and with her arms folded, she still looked good as ever. I swear she was the coldest brown skin in all New Orleans. I wasn't just saying that because we had history. Nah, I meant that shit. She stood before me wearing one of those sexy ass bodycon dresses with the strappy from Breathless Pandemonium Boutique, some bad ass heels. I could tell that her toes were freshly painted. She was even wearing my favorite color dope white as if she knew I would be coming home today. I swear I was a sucker for white manicured toes. Though she had naturally pretty long hair, she was now rocking a 30-inch silky straight weave. Everything about her glowed from her head to her toes.

And honestly, she would cross my mind every now and then while I was serving time in the pen. We had lost contact many years ago. It's crazy because I always swore that if I could bet my money on who would be the last person standing, it would always be Keke. She was the first person to jump ship, but she had her logical reasons. Shorty almost got caught with a major drug trafficking charge all because of me. I really couldn't be mad at her for finally choosing herself in the end because she held it down for too many years to count. So those years made up for it.

I swear as soon as I caught Keke looking over at me, my phone began vibrating in my pocket. Shit, when I went into the pen the iPhone 5S was out and now I was holding the iPhone XS Max. So much shit had changed, almost damn near evolved when I was in the pen. The person responsible for me having the latest iPhone was also the same chick that was blowing me up. I pulled out my iPhone XS

Max. I had several notifications ranging from missed phone calls, unread text messages, and even Instagram notifications. I'm sure they were all welcome home notifications. I'm sure I was probably New Orleans #1 trending topic on every social media platform there was. I swear I would always be that nigga no matter what. No matter if I had shackles around my ankles or not. Whenever Dollar 's name was mentioned in the N.O., I was bound to bring the whole city out, literally. It was to the point where people were turned around at the door due to capacity issues. All of this further boosted my ego. Dickriding hoes blows it.

I'm not going to lie, at first, I didn't plan on responding to Misha's texts in front of Keke's face. I just felt like that was too disrespectful but then I remembered that her best friend told off on her. I could tell by the way she twisted her face that she didn't want that kind of information getting out to me. It was cool though. On the outside that is, I was lowkey feeling salty. I knew what kind of woman Keke had been to me. I could only imagine the kind of person she had been to the ol' dude she was now with. Whoever he was, I wasn't trying to find out. Not right now at least. I needed to enjoy my first week of freedom at least. Though I was running shit in prison and behind Prison Walls, it was nothing like being able to sleep, shit and piss whenever you wanted to.

I peered at Keke one last time before reading my text messages from Misha.

"I'm sorry that I had to miss your big day, bae. You know I would have been there front row and center like I've always been for the last few years. Remember that," I read the text message out loud without looking at Keke. Although I was on some slick messy shit, I didn't want to make it that obvious. I just wanted her to feel slightly jealous like I did a few minutes ago. Clearly, she heard me too because I heard her grunt.

Sucking her teeth, she said, "Do you still want that apology? If so, I'm sorry for whatever you feel like I did to you. I'm ready to go home now."

" What's wrong? Is Boo blowing up your phone too?" I smirked for the hell of it, wanting to piss her off all over again."

I was expecting her to deny what I said because I knew she felt some type of way earlier. Instead she said, "Yup! I think both of our boos are hitting us up. Two exes should not be in the same room together especially not in such close proximity. We wouldn't want to give our boos the wrong impression, right?" she asked sarcastically before standing to her feet. I swear I never had an athletic bone in my body, but I jumped up like Steph Curry or some shit, nearly dropping the new phone on the marble floor in the process.

"Whoa, whoa, whoa. Just because we got some messages from our lil yeas, it does not mean that I gave you permission to go. I swear you think you're slick. Don't you realize Keke that this is way deeper than an apology right now? You and I have unfinished business. You feel me?"

Keke scrunched her face up. "What do you mean by unfinished business? Our business was done when you had to do a bid. That was so many years ago, I swear I lost count," she lied, forgetting that I could read her better than she could read her own damn self.

I pinned her by the waist so that she wasn't able to move. As uncomfortable as this conversation was already making her, it still didn't change the fact that we needed to talk about it."

"No, you the one that let a prison sentence cause thing to end between us. You wrote a nigga one time, telling me how you were changing your life around and that's it. I didn't hear from you any time after that. Hell, you probably thought I died or some shit."

"Nah, I didn't think you were dead. I'm 100% sure that would have made the paper and the news. However, I did think you were going to spend life in prison. I mean that is the sentence they gave you right?"

I looked at Keke as if she had lost her mind. "C'mon now. You know damn well they weren't about to actually make me serve life in prison. I'm the one that basically made junkies get off their asses and work to get another serving. C'mon now! They just wanted to make an example out of me for the motherfukers who thought they would be the next Dollar in these streets. That's it, that's all!"

"If that's it and that's all then let me go home. Damn," she huffed like a little kid, making me give in for a moment.

"You want to go home so bad then let's go home," I told her, practically picking her up and carrying her out the club. On the way out, I thanked the boss for letting us stick around after closed hours. He dapped me up and then said, "Handle that!"

"Trust me, I will!"

"No, he won't," Keke shouted. Because I would hate to have to handle his bitch!"

Hearing her say that made a nigga's dick hard. I should have been upset with Keke, but I loved her too much. She would never know that though. I carried her all the way to my new Mercedes truck. I swear by looking at me and seeing what I was rocking and driving, you wouldn't have known that I have served some years in the pen and was just now getting out. My granny and street brothers made sure I was straight the entire time. However, Misha mostly did too. I learned through my granny that she was the one that stayed on top of everyone to ensure that I had the latest and greatest once I got out.

Once Keke dipped out of the picture, I started entertaining Misha when I first went in. It was never supposed to be that way. In fact, I thought that the things I went through with Keke was supposed to keep us tied together forever but I was wrong. After shorty almost risked her freedom by almost catching a drug trafficking charge, that was the demise of our relationship. To make my money for a living, I had to depend on other people. Yeah, I was a grown ass man, but I still needed someone to depend on. Unfortunately, Misha was there the entire step of the way. Though I kept tabs on my ex, I never thought we would get back together or anything like that. So, she left me no other choice but to move on. The crazy thing is, I felt guilty now that I was out.

Part of me wanted to hold Misha down because she did the same for me. The other half of me wanted to take Keke to my new place and catch up on everything that has been happening with her. Also, I wanted to talk about the crazy shit I saw during my time locked up.

As sweet and loyal as Misha was, I couldn't connect with her like I did with Keke. All Misha was talking about is me coming out and becoming a reformed person. While I knew she meant well, this street was embedded in me. It was damn near part of my DNA. I didn't need anyone who wanted to change me. I needed someone that would accept me regardless of how I spent my free time and how I made my money. Misha wanted things for me that I didn't want for myself. Don't get me wrong I wasn't saying that Keke agreed with my actions either but if I needed her, she wasn't afraid to ride in the passenger side or help me move that weight. Whereas with Misha, I would probably have to kill her ass for snitching behind my back.

Basically, I wanted to continue my old lifestyle. Although I would be taking a backseat this time, I would still be in these streets. Truth be told, I simply couldn't trust Misha with my freedom the way I could in the past with Keke. And although Keke was currently giving me the cold shoulder, I knew she would come around eventually. Right now, I just needed to be patient with her. In the meantime, I would give Misha the time she gave me! "I see you managed your money well," Keke said as we walked towards my Mercedes truck. It was matte black on the outside with red seats on the inside. The seats had the King of New Orleans etched in the seats. You would probably think that people are overhyping me, but I swear, I was worth all the hype that I would get.

"You know my granny always said we were poor once and we weren't going back to being poor. She made sure of that while I was locked up. I trusted my boys with my life, but I only trusted my granny with my money."

She chuckled. "I haven't seen Ms. Bertha in forever! I used to love being around her." For the first time tonight, she finally cracked a genuine smile. I swear seeing her smile also made me smile even harder. I mean, I had already been smiling all day after finally being granted my freedom. I think we both had weak spots for each other that we were both fighting to show.

"You know you're more than welcome to come by anytime. Grandma B don't discriminate at all. She knows why you and I broke up. She doesn't fault you at all. I swear women are funny as hell. When y'all break up with the dude, y'all break up with the dude's whole family too. You know for yourself that Grandma has been nothing but nice to you. She treated you like you were her daughter," I laughed at her pettiness.

"I don't even want to be petty or intrusive. You got a new girl, so I don't want to be that type of girl. You know? I would hate to be hanging out at your Grandma's house and your new girl pop up unexpectedly with the shits."

"Damn I can see your heart beating out your chest. What are you scared for?" I joked. Out of nowhere, she playfully punched me in the arm.

"You want me to get out of character so bad. Don't you? Well too bad I'm not! I'm much better than that now. What I will say is this, I'm glad you're out. I can't tell a grown man what to do. I know it's hard to let go of that lifestyle, but I hope you stay under the radar."

Silence fell upon us as we drove around the city. Although it was late as hell it seemed like the party was still going on throughout the city. I drove around aimlessly until Keke said, "By the way, I need to give you my new address. It's been years and I no longer live in those apartments."

"Trust me I know," I let it slip out.
Out of the corner of my eye I could see her twist her neck. "And how exactly do you know? Nigga, you don't know if you want to be the Feds or Pablo Escobar," she joked.

"In this case, I'm Pablo Escobar and you are definitely the Feds!" I shot back for the hell of it.

"You want everyone to give you credit but it's hard for you to give other people credit. You know I ain't never snitch. I played my role and I played it well. I bet if you put another chick in my position she would have folded. The bitch wouldn't have had the guts and glory to stick around as long as I did. Now give me my fuckin' credit. The glowing illumination from the interior of the truck was lit to the point where I could see Keke holding her hand out as if she was just asking for some money.

"I'll give you your credit if you tell me one thing. Just one thing."

"And what's that?" she cut me off.

"Who is your new dude?"

Listen, I was kicking myself for asking that dumb ass question! Although I was curious, I shouldn't have let that come out of my mouth. Just like I knew she was curious about the chick I was texting earlier, but she didn't say anything. It was hard still caring about somebody after all this time has passed. What was even harder was pretending not to care when you really did.

"Remember what you used to tell me when you didn't think I was ready to know about your plugs and connections? Uhm, I don't think you're ready for me to disclose that kind of information just yet. Besides, he's a normal guy with a normal 9 to 5 just trying to make it. Let's not mix business with pleasure, shall we? I don't need you sending your goons after him just because we have something going on."

"I mean, I don't know who you're trying to convince at this point. You know damn well that you don't like normal ass guys. How could you downgrade to a normal ass guy after messing with someone like me? That doesn't even make sense. Plus, I can just see a normal guy not being your type. You will walk all over his ass if he isn't careful. C'mon now, Keke. You know damn well you ain't fucking with no lame, no nerd." Though we had history and I still had slight feelings for shorty, I was more disappointed in her poor taste more than anything else. Fuck her having a new dude. Right now, it was the type of dude she was fucking with that bothered me more than her having an actual dude. Crazy, I know. Well, nothing about our love was stable anyways. Not right now at least.

"I don't know how many times I have to tell you that I left my old life behind once the judge slapped you with that sentence. I don't get how you did that many years without coming out a changed ass dude. You're still caught up on slanging and having the keys to the streets and shit. Well listen, Dollar! I almost caught a charge behind your ass. What I won't do is almost catch another charge behind someone else. You taught me the game and I learned some valuable ass lessons from you the hard way! At this point, I'm only getting older and I need stability more than a nigga with street credit. So, hey! If that's lame to you, then it is what it is. At least I don't have to worry about our date nights being interrupted by the Feds raiding our spot," she threw so much shade. It was ridiculous.

About 5 years ago, we were celebrating our anniversary. That year, I planned to keep it simple yet special. So, I got in the kitchen and whipped up a lil' fancy meal I stumbled across on Facebook. I did that shit women be doing for men on Valentine's Day! Candles were lit, slow jams were playing in the background, rose petals were scattered throughout my condo. I had never done anything this romantic for Keke or any other woman in my life. I swear! Not even for my granny and as street as I was, I swear I was a grandma's boy at heart! That's how I knew Keke was mad special to me.

Anyway! Right before she was about to reward me with some pussy for my efforts on our special day, the fucking Feds raided my crib. We were both hauled out of there in cuffs. I made sure I hired the best Jewish lawyer in all of New Orleans. I told my lawyer straight up that he didn't have to defend me but he better not only defend the fuck out of Keke and get all possible charges dropped against her or that pretty little wife and two kids he had back at home would no longer have a damn space on Earth. I didn't give a fuck about myself in that moment because I always knew what the consequences of slanging and becoming a dope boy in these streets consisted of. You would either wound up dead or wound up in jail. Luckily for me, it was the latter! On top of that, I believed in facing everything like a man. I wasn't about to run from no crackers trying to throw away the key on me! How I see it is that I was to G for that shit!

Needless to say, all charges against Keke were dropped. And I was slapped with a life sentence. There were so many drug charges stacked against me. After I served a few years and got tired of being behind prison walls, I used the same Jewish lawyer from many years ago. Now I was free, and I planned on keeping it that way.

I mean you can sit up here and say that until you turn blue in the face. Remember that I've known you longer than that guy you're messing with. You like bad guys. A good dude can't do shit for you. Come on now you know you crave that hood love! What grandma used to say?"

"Hood love is that good love," we both responded at the same time, cracking up.

"Uhm, we did have some good times, right?" she asked, her voice fading with every word.

We both sat in the truck just reminiscing. "I probably made the mistake of letting you handle my dope with me. In fact, I know I did. However, I can say that you definitely had more good days in our relationship than you did bad days. Regardless of what was going on in the street, I made it my mission to always keep you safe and lace in the hottest shit. "Can't nobody in the city say that I had you out here looking crazy and busted! Man, hell nah! Gimme my fucking credit," I boasted.

I swear dudes loved to brag on they ratchet ass baby mamas, but I swear Keke had all of them beat and she wasn't even a baby mama. I couldn't help but smile as I thought about the old days. I swear we were a power couple in New Orleans at one point.

"I'll give you your credit for that. No matter if I had to get my hands dirty you can bet that my nails were done. My hair stayed laid and my outfits were always on point." she couldn't hide that big white smile even if she wanted to. I could see her smiling in the dark.

"I'm just curious though. I'm not even on some hating shit when I ask you this. But does he do it?"

She turned to face me. "Does he do what?"

Shrugging my shoulders, I said, "Shit, I don't know. Does he take care of your every need like I did? Does he make sure you're straight? If some shit were to pop off right now with him, would he put his life on the line for you? Other than his words, how do you know for certain?"

"I see where this is going, Dollar! All I got to say is not today and no time soon. The only place we need to be going is that address I gave you about 20 minutes ago."

"I'm like God around this bitch! I may not make you answer me now, but yo' ass sholl gon' have to answer me later!"

With that, I scratched my plans of taking Keke to my place and drove her ass home. I wanted to play my cards right. I needed to know where shorty head was at after all the shit that went down!

4:50 A.M.

For some strange reason, I woke up in the middle of my sleep thinking about Keke. I didn't know why considering that she was pretty much dismissive the entire time we were alone. She hardly engaged in any of my conversation. On top of that, a nigga was extremely horny. I rolled over and grabbed my Apple Watch off the night table since my iPhone had died completely once I finally closed my eyes.

Just before dozing off, I had been searching for Keke's social media accounts with no such luck. I just wanted to see if she was on Instagram living her best lie, I mean best life without me. At one point in our relationship, you never saw me and Keke without each other. The love she had for me and the love I have for her was completely unmatched.

Yeah, I fucked around with different chicks, but I made sure to do all of that behind her back. No one would have ever known that I was living a double life. My side chicks knew better. You know like how Jay Z mistress never revealed herself to Beyonce! That's because I only messed with bitches who knew they would have a lot to lose if they were to ever open their mouths. I'm not talking about no job, no money, no cars or no shit like that. When I said they had something to lose, I was talking about their life. I didn't play this snitching shit period. I don't care whether it was street or nonstreet related!

Since I had been locked up and the special visits, they would let me get were far and in between, I went back to who had been there for the last few years. Misha! Even though it was super late as hell, I knew she would still be up. So, I hit her up, wanting to relieve some pent-up pressure. Honestly, seeing Keke is what really had me through the roof right now. Had she been single, I probably would have tried to make a move on her tonight. That cold shoulder she was giving me told me she wasn't fucking with me right now. So, I had no other choice but to fuck with who I know was currently fucking with me the long way. I sent one emoji to see if she was up. I swear Misha didn't even give me type to exit off her message before it lit up.

Late night tip? Great minds think alike, I see. The text read.

Hell yeah! Go wake that lil' pussy up. Go freshen up, throw some water on it or some shit. I'll be on my way in within the next hour or so. I responded then I got up to take a quick shower and brush my teeth.

I swear bitches would do anything when you were that nigga. Here it was at this time of morning and I was about to slide up in a chick who wasn't even my official girl or anything like that.

About an hour later, I pulled up to Misha's spot and locked my truck doors. Her door came swinging open as if she was standing by the door and waiting for me to pull up on her. Shawty stood before me and greeted me with absolutely nothing on. I mean, there wasn't even a robe, not even those body stockings she wore underneath her regular visitation clothes. I knew she couldn't wait, and neither could I since I had to relieve myself damn near every night with no assistance, but she could've at least respected herself enough to cover that shit up.

If she was my official girl, then there was no way in hell I was about to allow her to open the door naked, giving the whole fucking hood a full view of what's supposed to be mine. I swear it seemed like every time I fucked with a bitch, she showed me why she was nothing more than a fuck to me. Only one woman had come close to making me wife her and she still didn't even know that shit to this day!

"What's good, zaddy," she purred as she led the way down her long corridor. All you could see was her big round, caramel colored ass jiggling and the clacking of her "Fuck Me" heels against her cheap marble ass floors.

"Hold on now, Misha! This my first time in your spot and you ain't telling me where we are going?" I inquired like a detective when I noticed that we were no longer in her living room. "If I'm not mistaken, the sectional is back that way, we actually already passed that mothafucka."

See? These are the kind of things that happened when you got distracted by butt naked ass hoes. This particular kind of distractions right here would have you forgetting to put the rubber on and then wondering why the chick turned up pregnant two weeks later or worse – have you inside the damn clinic with some burns! Now that I was officially from behind bars, I needed to buckle down and focus. I literally couldn't afford any distractions in my personal or business life. I had to make up for years' worth of lost time!

"Damn Dollar! Why are you acting like this? You clearly said you want some pussy and I desperately want some of that freedom dick! Nigga, I let you fuck me in that cold ass room, on that cheap, metal ass bed. For the past few years at that too! So, let's not be picky now! Besides, ain't nobody in here! Why would I have you going back to prison with a murder charge? I'm not stupid, Dollar! I want you to enjoy your freedom and I also want to enjoy it with you. Can we please take this to the bedroom?" she whined.

At this very moment, I gave her the signature look Ike Turner would've given Tina Turner had she questioned him like that. "First off, you chose to get fucked on that small ass bed. I never asked you to become my prison slut. You volunteered to become one. If it's a problem, remember that I can always go back to the one I started with."

Misha spun on her heels and turned to face me. "I just hope you ain't referring to Keke," she said with attitude while sucking her teeth. Although I was thinking that, she said the magic words. Shorty had now gotten in front of me and we were now heading back to the couch. She didn't like the idea of having competition. I mean, all women were like that.

However, Misha would go above and beyond to make sure she outdid Keke. I think it's because everyone knew how Keke held it down without me having to say a word. Misha got inspired to do the same but she lowkey turned that shit into an obsession. It seemed like the closer it came time for me to get out, she amped things up a bit. Like the whole truck thing, the phone, and other things. Though they were sweet gestures, I know they truly weren't genuine. Secretly, she wanted to outdo Keke. Little did Misha know, buying material things wouldn't be the way to outdo her. Cause what Keke did was way riskier and more complicated than filling out some damn paperwork to make sure I got a car and a new phone! Misha was older than all of us combined, but she was too simple-minded. With me wanting to get back knee-deep in the drug game, I really couldn't have someone like Misha by my side. She would be trying to take my money and spend it on material shit. Shit that would lose value the next day. However, she was the only attention I had at the moment. Why fuck shit up?

After what seemed like an eternity, Misha finally got on the couch and got down on all fours, giving me full access to her ass and fat pussy. I can't lie, all her shit looked good from the back. Just looking at her shit reminded me of that fat, juicy caramel cake that my grandma used to bake for the church on Sundays! She began to put on a show as she rubbed her clit while I undressed and put a Magnum on.

Now that I was out, I could suppress my urges much better than I did behind those prison walls. That meant strapping the fuck up like I was supposed to. I came behind her and slowly inserted my dick inside of her soaking, wet kitty. Misha's pussy was usually a 7.5 or quite average because it had been around the block and throughout the city a few times. Yeah, I knew shorty wasn't as innocent as she pretended to be. They never were! But right now, she was at a good fucking ten on a scale of one to ten. Trust me the small details she was usually lacking with her pussy game, you better believe that her mouth made up for it. She was moaning obnoxiously and clawing at the satin pillows on the sectional.

"Damn, Dollar ...Dollar," Misha kept moaning out my name as I quickly moved in and out of her.

I couldn't believe that a nigga could finally get some pussy whenever and most importantly wherever again. Maybe I needed to wait a little longer before I touched her again because it seemed like she had only gotten tighter and wetter with time. "Fuckkk...I'm about to cum, Dollar," she yelled, nearly waking her neighbors up in the process, which caused me to pick up my pace expeditiously.

"Fuck, me too, girl. Say, tell me where you want this nut?" I asked her in a low, raspy tone.

"Baby, I want it in my mouth," she moaned sexily as I hurriedly pulled out of her kitty. She quickly dropped to the floor and opened her mouth wide as my seeds spurted out as if it were a water hose filling up a pool or some shit. She was indeed a nasty, thirsty bitch right about now. She probably had so many of my babies in her mouth right now, I just knew her throat was probably clogged up.

Visibly, I could see that she swallowed, but I had to make sure she swallowed every last drop. Bitches were always finding new ways to trap you even if you weren't finishing inside of them. Like I said, it was time re-up and let mothafuckas know the real king was home. I didn't need no potential baby momma news coming within the next two weeks or so. I was already locked down via handcuffs. The last thing I needed was her and a baby trying to lock me down a well.

"Open up your mouth now and say ahh," I demanded, not giving one single fuck.

"Ahh," she opened her mouth wide as if she was at the dentist office getting checked for cavities. I saw no remnants of my nut as she literally swallowed all of it, so we were good for now. I took the condom inside the kitchen and threw it down her garbage disposal before washing my hands. Yeah, it wasn't no digging in the trash for the condom when I left. Nah! I put that mothafucka in the sink and let the blades handled it. When I returned to the living room, Misha was sprawled out on the couch, slowly rubbing her kitty in a circular motion. I swear she was dramatic as hell. After being pounded out by so many different men, I don't see how she could still get so damn sore down there. Then again, a nigga's weight did go to his dick. On top of that, I was already 6'2.

Not wanting to linger around after getting my fix, I began to put back on my clothes and grabbed my keys off her coffee table. "Good fucking game! I'll probably see you within the next few weeks or so. I don't know yet right now."

She shot up from the couch. "Next few weeks? You don't know? Uh, c'mon now, Dollar! See? Something told me that you immediately switch up once you were actually released. I can already tell that our time spent together will now be at a minimum. I don't even know why I believed those lies you told me when you were locked up. I think I know what it is too. You saw Misha at the club tonight, huh? Let me guess! Your old feelings somehow managed to come back. Now you're about to start back fooling with her because she supposedly "held you down". Is that what it is, huh?" With the way she asked the question, you would've thought she knew that it was time for me to go back to my old lifestyle. Sometimes that meant going back to the person you already knew too. She didn't have to know that Keke wasn't feeling me right about now nor did she have to know any answers to the many questions I could see her coming up with inside her head.

"You got the dick you wanted, right? Exactly! Then don't worry about who's getting it next! Don't worry about all of that. Just play your part, Misha."

"Who said anything about playing a part? If anything, I want to be the leading lady. Fuck playing a part! Remember that I held it down when you were behind those bars. Anybody can hold you down when you have freedom. Those are usually the first people to run as soon as you get locked up though. Yes, she held you down before all of this shit happened. After everything went down who was there? It was me," she began to slightly yell while hitting her chest.

"No matter what I do, I can never get any real credit from you. It seems like she gets all the credit because she held a few drugs or something. You up here acting like you had a young Griselda Branco. You said you're getting back into their lifestyle, right? What do you need me to do? Ride around the city in your passenger with weed baggies on me? Is that all it takes to get your full and undivided attention? To me, that seems like doing minimum. I guess I'm fine with it. I mean you seem to praise people that do the bare minimum anyways!"

I chuckled at her. "Keke got your ass pressed like a panini and you don't even know her personally. You only character based off all the good things I've said about her. That's wild to me. Maybe get some confidence and I probably would stick around. You too damn pretty for that hating shit!" And she truly was! Shorty reminded me of somebody that would be considered Instagram famous due to her pretty, flawless face and curvy figures that she didn't have to go to

Miami for. It was clearly that she envied Keke and I wasn't fucking with that. I liked my women with confidence. I didn't have time to be babying a grown ass woman especially over another grown ass woman. Not wanting to waste my time arguing with her because I needed some rest and due to the fact that were weren't officially together, I walked out of Misha's spot and headed back home to catch up on some well-needed sleep before my first day out business meeting.

***

CHAPTER 3:

JAZZY JACOBS
ONE NIGHT

Imagine after a long night of smoking, drinking and vibing with someone else, having to come home to a nagging ass, insecure ass partner. Unfortunately, this was currently the story of my life right about now. After I left the nightclub with Dollar 's prison friend, Draco, we went to his lil' townhouses and smoked that shit completely out.

As much sexual tension there was between us last night, neither of us acted on it. Honestly, I was too damn scared to fuck with niggas who had served long sentences. From what Draco told me, he served twelve years due to a murder charge that occurred back in his late adolescent years. Since I always had a thing for dudes in the hood, the murder charge isn't what had me side-eyeing Draco. In every hood, you had that one dude they either had a murder assault or robbery charge. I just felt like that came with dating hood niggas. I just didn't want to fuck a nigga until I saw his clinic test results. Not that I had anything against gay men, but I was not about to let a bi-ass dude stick his dick in me. Especially not one that has been in jail that long. I didn't have enough information about him to know his definite sexual orientation. Although I didn't get any questionable vibes from him only time would be able to reveal certain things to me.

BOOM!

That was the sound of an entire set of custom orders hitting the floor simultaneously.

"I swear if you broke my client's shits, I'm going to beat your ass all throughout this house and outside of it too," I threatened as I walked into the living room wanting to assess the damages. My major client's projects set off to the side of the room completely untouched which was a good thing. For many months now, I have been trying to get into handmade crafts. The hair, makeup and lashes market were way too overcrowded for me. I was now looking for ways to make passive income and I was finally starting to enjoy the fruits of my labor.

"Obviously you wanted my attention. Instead of communicating like a grown ass woman, you would rather throw tantrums and our fucking bill money! Now you have my attention, try to keep it. What the fuck is up, Tonya?" I asked my annoying ass girlfriend.

"Shit, that's what I need you to tell me. That's what I'm trying to figure out now. I tried to go out of my so-called selfish ways and do something nice for a change. Your trifling ass didn't even show up until this morning, completely disregarding all of my efforts," she pouted, which definitely wasn't a good look on her considering this tough character she tried to portray.

Tonya was my part-time girlfriend for a little over a year now. Truth be told, I don't know how we made it to a year after all this bickering and breaking up we were doing. In the beginning, she gave me the rapper Yung MA vibes. She was the perfect mix between a little girly and a little tomboy, which I could definitely deal with.

At one point, she had a feminine look about herself that I loved. She was a pretty mixed chick with long, off brown hair and big brown eyes. She wasn't super skinny nor was she super thick either. She was simply just right. Just right for me, I thought. That was then but now was a completely different story. She had gone from looking like Yung Ma to Queen Latifah in Set It Off real damn quick. Her weight had begun to increase drastically. She no longer had a soft, feminine look about herself. She straight up carried herself like a hobo ass dyke.

Her once straight, pretty hair stayed in two, frizzy braids that were braided to the back. Now, she always wore different color bandanas as a headband. She even had the nerve to now sag and dracoss in baggy clothes. Basically, she had let herself go, which caused me to lose interest in her in return. Her image had gotten so bad that I could no longer do my part and please her in the bedroom. Now she had to do all of the pleasuring while I had the privilege to be on the end of receiving.

The crazy thing is, sex was now very limited with us too. What did it look like my fine ass squeezing on some big o titties that belonged to a chick that acted and now looked like a boy? Just the visual alone had me ready to throw up in my mouth. When I dated bitches, I wanted pretty bitches. Don't get me wrong! Yung Ma was a tomboy too, but she definitely kept up with her appearance way better than Tonya! When I dated dudes, I wanted hardcore ass dudes. Tonya was trying too damn hard to be Tony and that wasn't working for me.

I rolled my eyes at her constant lies which was also another problem. "Really, Tonya? What exactly did you have planned out for me? Nothing looks out of the ordinary in here other than this damn house looking like a toddler ran through it."

She shoved her phone in my hand, which I couldn't help but notice that was set on 'Do Not Disturb'. Yep, I paid attention to the small things as well. I looked at the photos that were taken at a new restaurant that recently opened here. Surprisingly, there was a candlelight dinner set up. My favorite pink and white roses were also placed on each side of the tabletop along with a small blue bag from Tiffany & Co. Almost instantly, I felt guilty as I did remember Tonya constantly blowing up my phone last night. Too bad I had already planned to celebrate our city's special day and the secret release of Dollar. The entire city knew about this day, so it wasn't my fault her insecure ass purposely chose this day to "celebrate" our "relationship". This a calculated move on her behalf.

"Uhm, I'm sorry. That's all I got for ya." That was all I could muster up right about now.

Tonya snatched the phone out of my hand, then backed up against the dining room table. "So, that's all you have to say huh? Just sorry with no explanation? No thank you? No reason as to why you ignored my calls? Huh? Nothing!"

My eyes were now squinted due to confusion. "Do I really owe you an explanation because I truly feel like I don't owe you anything at all. I have already said sorry. I mean, what more do you want me to say?"

"You could at least thank me for my efforts or hell, you could make an effort to reschedule our date night. You would much rather be nonchalant right about now."

Now Tonya was extra bugging and shit. "Do you really wanna talk about effort right now? Your effort came a little bit too late if you ask me. Where was all of this effort a few months ago when I needed you to take us seriously? You were too busy overlooking me and fucking with those other bitches who were boosting your damn ego. Now that you've put on all of this weight and ya' ass is no longer popping to these dusty ass hoes; you want to do right by me. Nah, fuck all that Tonya. Although it was a really nice gesture of you, the candlelight dinners and the pretty, expensive flowers came a little bit too late. That's all!"

I walked out of the kitchen and headed to my bedroom where Tonya was right on my heels.

"Baby...Jazzy," she called behind me. "I'm sorry I didn't appreciate you when I first got you. I was too busy sweating these other girls that I forgot about you in the process. I don't want to lose you! I'm serious this time around."

The sight of her begging disgusted me. She was way too grown to be acting like this. I glanced at her outfit. She was rocking a red, loose fitting tee with those camouflage cargo shorts I couldn't stand. She paired the outfit with her favorite, icy white Nike Air Force Ones. Of course, there was a camouflage bandana tied around her head, making her look like a complete fool. I wondered what she'd seen looking back at her in the mirror. My thing is, why date a woman who carried herself like a man when I could just go be with a real man? When I pursued lesbians, they were the kind who you would never suspect were carpet munchers. They carried themselves like ladies, which I loved. I didn't have anything against those who carried themselves like men, they just weren't my type. That's all.

"Damn Tonya, please get yourself together. Go to a spa, groom your nails and hair or something. I simply need a break right now," I finally admitted, although the break was long overdue. However, being around Draco last night had confirmed how much I wanted to go back to the other side for a while. Even if it wasn't with him exactly, I needed to try dating men again.

"Well fuck you too then, Jazzy! You expect the entire world to kiss the ground that you walk on and beg your ass for the time of day. Hoe, you ain't special! You damn sure ain't the only one trying to be the only, anyway!"

I laughed at her because I was so damn unbothered. "Oh, I'm content with not being any number at all. That's basically what I'm trying to get you to understand. It's over, it's done. I'll get up with you later though."

Tonya shook her head then left my apartment. As soon as she did, I decided to hit up Draco. I was officially about to start back making dick appointments. But first, I needed him to go get tested with me so that I could ease my mind

***

CHAPTER 4:
DRACO THOMAS
ISSA SETUP

Since Draco was so called recovering from his special release turn-up, we enjoyed a nice day away from the office aka our trap house. Despite being in the pen, I was handling all of the communication for Dollar. Even inside, that nigga had a group of solid niggas that would put their life on the line for him. I'm not going to lie, within those last years we were in the joint together, he really enhanced my family's life. Although I wasn't officially with my baby momma, I would do anything to make sure she and my kids were straight.

"Yo, why are you up here cheesin' like that? You must get some of that here-kitty-kitty from Jazzy's cocky ass last night?" Dollar asked me.

We were currently chilling inside of my new apartment that I was able to get thanks to Dollar, smoking blunts and sipping on a few drinks. Henny thing possible.

I laughed. "Nah, shorty didn't give it up last night. We were on some straight vibing shit even though I could tell she wanted to bust it open for a nigga. I love it when you know a chick is an undercover freak, but she tries to disguise it. I think she was a little skeptical of the whole prison thing. You could tell by the way she kept asking me questions about prison but trying to dance around certain questions."

"Fuck that! Not all of us go in there to bend over and get cracked. Shit, we served our time, fucked our female visitors when we could and served our time. Don't worry though. It's going to happen sooner rather than later. Jazzy looked like she was ready to risk it all for you in the club. I was saying in my head, shorty doesn't know what she's getting her ass into. You better tell her not to fuck around and play with you. You ain't scared to catch a body," Dollar teased.

"Listen I told her straight up last night that I am not with the shits! I am not one of those dudes you can punk out and walk all over. I could tell by the way she was dissing her ex that she is a real work of art. Man; I've calmed down a bit, but I am not with that disrespectful shit. Don't disrespect me and I won't disrespect you. Cuz I be trying to tell people that they won't like how I disrespect them back. So, before we have to shoot it out, I just prefer for that person to watch their mouth from the start.

I ended up getting a long sentence for killing a tourist for disrespecting my first baby mama at the time. Dude was talking out the side of his neck without even noticing that I heard him the whole time. As soon as he was about to get in his cab to go wherever, I ran up on him and started dumping on him. Was it worth it in the end? I really couldn't say. What I will say is this, my baby mamas were no longer struggling to make ends meet once I got locked up. That's because Dollar and I developed a bond. He paid me to run his business from the inside to the outside.

"Yeah, you definitely got to keep those two in their places or they will try you as if you're a bitch or something."

"I'm already knowing. However, I don't mind putting up with a little bit of drama if the person is worth it. But what's up with you and Keke? Y'all argued so much last night. I'm sure y'all made up after she was forced to stay behind. I bet shorty really thought she would be able to go home once we all left."

Hell yeah, she really did. I haven't seen that beautiful face in 5 years and she really thought she was about to get away from me. Hell nah! I wanted to hold her hostage back in my place, but she was tripping. So, I finally took her home and decided to link up with Misha."

"Aw shit! How did that go? Is she still pressuring you for more?"

Man, it's the same shit, just a different damn day. I don't think that women understand that we don't move on their time. All of that rushing only slows down the process. She won't be getting her expected outcome with me anyways. I'm not even attracted to her like this. I don't know why but I can just see Misha setting me up or something.

Aw hell, then you already know what that means. You gotta cut shorty off. Listen I already said I'm not going back to the pen for nobody else. I just want to make some money and enjoy my freedom. You feel me? Besides always feel like Misha was just something to do because there literally was nothing else to do. That's how I feel about Paris too. I just needed some consistent pussy while being locked up!"

"I 100 percent feel you! She definitely would not be someone I will look at if I weren't Behind Bars. No offense cause shorty ain't hot at all!"

You are apologizing like I should be offended or something. Hell nah! That ain't my bitch. She was already clingy when I was locked up and now, she's even more clingy as hell. She won't stop blowing a nigga up."

"She fell in love with that prison dick, I swear," Dollar cracked up, but I didn't find shit funny about an old ass woman not knowing when to back the hell off. Now that I was out after a long ass time, I wasn't thinking about shorty at all. In fact, I was ready for something new. I had my eyes on Jazzy for the moment. It wasn't because she was the first chick, I actually held a conversation with once I was finally released. Nah, shorty was cold as fuck.

She reminded me of a prettier version of Joseline Hernandez without the crazy accent and all of that. I could see myself getting to know her better somewhere down the line. First, I needed to get my personal life together with my kids' mothers before seriously dating someone again. Either way it goes, I knew I was done fucking with

Paris. She was old enough to be my mom's oldest child or something. She was a cougar compared to me. And when I was hitting that pussy, her shit couldn't even latch on to my dick, I swear! She was a guard and we began messing around behind the authorities backs, of course. I don't know what made her push up on a nigga out of all people in the pen, but she did. At the time, I enjoyed getting sex even if it wasn't like the sex I used to get before being locked up. Some pussy was better than no pussy at all. And behind prison walls, old, worn down coochie was better some damn dick! I tell you that!

Dollar was still laughing as the phone continued to ring. "Just answer this one time. See what she wants! She may have some good news for you."

Sucking my teeth, I said, "What kind of good news could she possibly have for me? I'm already free! That's the best news I will ever get in my entire life span. This is our first and last conversation. I can promise you that!"

"Man, what do you want, Paris?" I answered, unable to mask my annoyance. She was so damn annoying to me already. I really didn't want to answer but I would much rather she kill my vibe right now than kill it later.

"This some fuck ass shit right here. So now you want to answer my phone call? I know you saw me calling you for the past few minutes in a row," she began to nag without my damn consent. See, giving her dick made her think she could talk to me any kind of way. I wasn't feeling that shit at all!

"I'm not even about to entertain you. My shackled days are over, and I no longer have to sit up and listen to this shit. It was fun while it lasted and now it's over! Bye, Paris." I was about to hang up until I heard, "Please Draco, this is a real serious matter."

"What, Paris? Say anything to get my attention!"

"Uhm, I think. I think I may be...fuck it...I'm p-p-pregnant," she stuttered and stammered all over her words.

"Hold up! You fu-fu-fuckin-w-wh-what?" I yelled so loud, I almost forgot that Dollar was inside causing him to slightly jump a bit.

"I'm pregnant, Draco," she repeated as if I didn't hear her the first time. "I'm pregnant!"

"Since when and how? Nah, I don't believe this shit right here. You just saying this because you know it's time for me to cut your ass off. That's it. That's all," I said, really trying to convince myself that I couldn't have knocked up a fucking prison guard.

"What do you mean when and how? Obviously, I got pregnant because you wouldn't stop fucking me in the laundry room of the damn prison. Nigga, you even fucked me when I was on my period. You back in the real world and you seem to have forgotten that the real world has consequences too, Draco! I'm sure it happened three weeks ago. Matter of fact, it was exactly three weeks ago because we had sex on my super fertile days," she recalled. It's almost as if I could hear the bitch smiling on the other end. Them inconvenient baby mommas sure loved carrying a baby that you didn't want!

"What the fuck? I only needed you as my cum disposal and nothing more," I corrected her. "What's crazy to me is how you remember the exact day it happened and shit. You knew you were ovulating, and I feel like you trapped me. I should be asking your ass which exact round it was to cause you to trap me since you can recall the small details and shit! What's your damn address? I'm about to come through!"

She recited her address and I damn near hung up while she was talking. Hopefully the bitch had enough common sense to text me the address. She sure didn't have enough sense to make sure she didn't get knocked up by someone who was young enough to her own damn son.

I ended the call to find Dollar looking up at me with a smirk on my face, as if he already knew what was up.

"Just confirm it! Your ass just got caught slipping, huh? She knew it was getting closer to that freedom and she wanted to be able to take some of it from you."

"That's what she claims. Man, I don't know for sure, bro. I mean, what if she another prison bae? What if she had a man at home the entire time? Shit like that!"

And that's why I feel like these are all the things you need to be asking her. Figure out what's going on and shit. You only get answers to the questions you ask. If she says it's your baby, then you need to get the proper proof. Don't take her word for it. Do you feel me? For all we know, the entire prison population could have been getting some of that. You can only trust these bitches as far as you can throw them. You didn't get to see her outside of prison, so you don't know for sure. But I mean if it's yours then handle your business. If not, then tell her to go find the right baby daddy."

"It's just crazy how she hit me with that news when I was just saying that I was feeling Jazzy. It's literally like something alerts women when you're on some other shit that does not involve them."
"I know it I know it. I think we both broke the rules when it came to dealing with these women in prison. We needed a way to relieve our urges without that homosexual shit. Now look at us. We have two women that we can't get off our backs."

"You in this one alone boss. I know how to get rid of my problem if need be."

" Come on now! I know you're enjoying this New Freedom. Don't let her be the reason why you get sent back. You won't get lucky and get out this time around. Think logically and use your common sense. Besides, you don't even know all the facts right now. You're just relying on her words which could be her way of being petty and trying to get next to you. Just calm down and go see what's up for now. That's all you can do right now."

Although I was a grown ass man, Dollar was right about now. I couldn't let a prison guard be the reason I go back in. Even if it was my child, I would do what I'm legally required to do and that's it. Other than that, it was fuck Paris. I had no business getting involved with her old ass anyway. Especially if she didn't know she still needed to be on fucking birth control.

He did try to warn me about messing with a prison guard, but I didn't listen. Dude was getting special visits and I wanted those special visits too. I had been in the system way longer than he had been. Despite Paris' age, she had the looks and body of a 20-year-old to me. It didn't help that she could make a nigga shake like a washer when I would have her beat over in the pen's laundry room where I worked part-time. Well, I worked in the laundry room alright. I used that low paying job to fuck with her that's it. Dollar made sure I was taken care of, so I didn't need the pennies they were paying me, but my penis needed some pussy so hey! Simply put, Paris was like the 35-year-old version of Angela Bassett but slightly less attractive than Angela. So, what the fuck did it look like a 26-year-old knocking her up?

"I really wouldn't let it bother me. No offense but just because she got a baby, it does not mean you have to be with her. She wanted a baby so bad, then make her ass raise it alone if she decides to keep it. All I can say is, tell her what it is and what it ain't. She has no other choice but to take into account how you feel. If wisdom really comes with age, then she will do the right thing. Ain't nobody trying to raise no kid alone nowadays. Well, I hope not! Our asses been locked up so shit, I can't really speak too much on that. Just let me know what happens."

"You've already said enough! Thank you, bro. I'm about to go ahead and handle everything now." I stood up from the couch. As comfortable as I was, I really didn't feel like moving. Too bad I had to go nip this shit in a bud ASAP. I wish I would've listened to you back then, but that's why I'm not claiming her baby right now. I'm about to continue on with my new freedom and tonight's plans until I'm able to do a blood test," I reassured him.

Although I was trying to play like I was cool, I truly wasn't. I really hoped like hell that I hadn't put a baby in Paris. That meant I would have to have dealings with her until she turned about 60 and I turned 42 or something. To my own stupidity, I didn't even think shorty could even produce a baby at that old ass age. My first stop would be to Walmart and Target to grab a few pregnancy tests that I needed her to take in front of me. That's for sure. It wasn't no buying prank pregnancy tests on me! Hell nah!

***

Once Dollar finally left, I headed over to Paris' crib to see what was up with this whole baby ordeal shit. The whole unexpected pregnancy announcement had me more bothered than I had initially let on to him. All a nigga wanted to do is take advantage of the opportunities that I didn't have prior to going to prison. Dollar had my entire family finally eating good, so I really didn't want to throw another mouth into that equation! Hell, I already had enough mouths to feed. I had two baby mommas and 3 kids. So, to hear Paris hit me with that kind of news, it definitely left me blindsided. A nigga definitely wasn't trying to raise a 4th child. I had been locked up so long. I felt like a kid finally being let out at recess. Why would I want to ruin the risk of raising another child when I felt like a child right now myself? It didn't make sense to me.

I grabbed both the Walmart and Target bags that ranged from regular pregnancy tests to the digital ones. Not exaggerating a bit, she was going to take all of them right in front of me. No questions asked! Forget taking it with first-morning urine. I needed whatever piss she could squeeze out right now.

She had the nerve to reach out for a hug as I got closer to her. "Hi, Draco."

I dodged her hug and went straight into the living room with the bag in my hand.

"Here yo' wannabe pregnant ass goes," I tossed the bag to her. She fumbled the bag just like she would also be fumbling the bag if she thought having this baby would be a come up or something.

"What's this?" she inquired while looking inside the bag. She had a frown on her face. Though Paris still looked pretty decent, without her makeup, she looked about 5 years older. In this moment, I realized how crazy the situation was from the start. This felt like I was faced to face with an aunt or something. I had no business letting her seduce me, period!

"Oh! So, you don't trust me now?" she finally asked. "Let's remember that I'm not the one that was doing a fucking bid! You were."

"It's not about trust because we didn't have anything that required trust in the first damn place. I just know how trifling women can be when they want something that they can't have. I think we both know that you can't have me. If you're pregnant like you claim that you are, then it shouldn't be a problem taking these pregnancy tests, right?"

She huffed around like a little ass kid. "Whatever, Draco! So, I take it that my word isn't enough? Why would I lie about a pregnancy? It's crazy how you trusted me enough to go raw inside of me but you can't trust my word about being pregnant. My word should be my damn bond, period."

My phone vibrated in my pocket. More than likely it was Jazzy texting me because I made last minute plans to see her in a bit. No matter what these hundred pregnancy tests would indicate, it wasn't about to ruin my day. I would have to just revisit that shit at a later date. "Look, just take the tests. It's simple! Plus, I have other things I need to do."

She stared at me in disbelief, as if she were genuinely shocked by my behavior. "I truly figured this would happen."
"Figured what would happen? Me being upset? Hell yeah, I'm upset. I have every right to be upset. I just feel like we're both too

damn old to be having ulterior motives. I was upfront about what I wanted from you. Too bad you couldn't be. Like I said, let's go take these damn tests right now."

I followed her as she headed to the bathroom. Though my anger was currently messing with my vision, I had to give her credit. Her spot was actually tidy. Whether she cleaned up because she knew I was coming over, now that was another story. Once we reached the bathroom, she tried to go inside and close the door behind her.

"Hold up! Why are you trying to run in there and close the door? I need to see you take these tests. Ain't no pulling no fake positive test on me. I just hope your grown ass ain't trying to hide that pussy when I've seen that pussy in every condition imaginable by now," I chuckled through my anger.

I watched intently as she grabbed a small bathroom cup from underneath the sink and sat on the toilet. I literally had to control the urge to blink out of fear that she may try to pull a fast one over on me. I mean, it was pretty evident at this point that she couldn't be trusted.
"Damn it!" she cursed out loud. "Do you mind handing me another cup from under the sink? This one just fell down in the toilet."

Going underneath the sink, I was about to grab the last lil' cup until something next to the cup caught my full attention. I pulled out the huge bottle of pills and examined it.

I held the pills up to her face, nearly wanting to hit her dead in her eyes with the bottle. "Yo, what the fuck is this?"

She looked shook as hell just a little bit. You can tell that she forgot that she had placed them there. It's not like I knew I would be coming over but I'm glad that I did. "Uhm pills...they're pills for women."

I shook the bottle for the hell of it. "Duh, these are some fucking pills. They damn sure aren't candies and shit like that. Why are you taking some damn fertile supplements at your age? Shouldn't you be preparing for menopause and not a damn baby?"

Paris tried to take the pills away from me but couldn't because I was stronger than her. "You don't even know what those are for. Besides, you don't even know when I bought those."

"Like hell I do. I'm not some young, dumb ass nigga. I know what fertile supplements are and the purpose of them! These are some damn fertility and prenatal pills combined, which means you real deal fucking trapped me on purpose. And according to how fresh this seal looks, I bet I can tell when you bought these. They had to have been purchased recently. I can tell you that. The question is why are you buying stuff like this? Why would you even want a baby considering the harsh environment you work in? You clearly letting a wet pussy take away your common sense!"

Filled with blind rage, I threw the pill bottle just a bit past her head and stormed out of the bathroom. Paris followed closely with the pregnancy tests in her hand. I damn near wanted to say fuck those tests at this point. I mean, it was obvious that shorty was pregnant if she was taking medication to assist in getting pregnant.

"So, um. I take it that you don't want to watch me take these pregnancy tests now?"

I couldn't believe she had the nerve to ask me something like that. The fact that she didn't deny trying to trap me was absurd as hell too. Paris was way too old to be pulling a stunt like this. I was still young as hell and fresh out of the fucking feds of all places. I hadn't even reached my thirties yet, so if she thought this was going to make me settle down with her, then she was definitely wrong. The crazy thing is, what if I didn't gain my freedom? I hope like hell she didn't think that I would be able to be actively involved in that child's life from behind some damn bars!

"Why would I want you to take a pregnancy test after knowing what I know now? Hell, I'm pretty positive your ass is pregnant now. Yo, I'm out."

The only reason I wanted to leave is that I was pissed. I didn't want to hurt Paris so I figured that it would be best to leave while I still had a little bit of sense in me. Like Dollar told me, it wasn't worth going back to jail over.

"Really, Draco? This is how you're going to act? What did you expect to happen if we were sleeping together unprotected?"

"I didn't expect your ass to want to trap a dude that was possibly serving a life sentence at the time, that's for sure. Yeah, it takes two people to fuck and it damn sure takes two people to raise a child. We consented to fuck each other, but we both didn't consent to get you knocked the hell up," I spat. "Any real woman of substance wouldn't be trying to raise an inmate's baby. That's for sure!"

"Whatever, goodbye, Draco."

"Exactly, Paris. Make sure you stay in this same lil' mood until I'm able to take a DNA test. Don't come my fucking way unless you don't want to go full-term with your pregnancy," I threatened her. "I kid you the fuck not!"

My threat would turn into a promise if need be. I didn't give a fuck about Paris as is. So, of course, I didn't give a fuck about a baby that could've easily been someone else's. These bitches weren't loyal, so I knew damn well their pussies weren't either. The crazy part is that we only slept without condoms occasionally. Yeah, I was stupid and desperate for pussy at the time. It's partially my fault, but Paris was also to blame as well. She was older than me, so she shouldn't have been on her bird behavior.

I walked out of Paris's crib still pissed as hell. I hated that I had to cancel my plans with Jazzy tonight but with the way I was feeling, I had no other choice. I wasn't in the mood to be around bitches. Right now, all bitches were public enemy #1.

***

CHAPTER FIVE:
KEKE JONES
STILL IN LOVE WITH MY EX

One Week Later

After a consistent week of blowing my phone up unrelentless, I finally agreed to let Dollar take me out on a friendship date or whatever that is. I can't lie, I was a bit nervous. It had been a minute since I went out on a date with Dollar. Plus, I was scared as hell that the same Juju would come back on us. Just my luck we would be sitting in the middle of the restaurant and that restaurant would get raided. Jazzy reassured me that I was over exaggerating, but I don't know. The thing with Dollar is that he was always unpredictable.

You never knew what was coming next with him. Since Taylor and I were on a mini break in our relationship, I finally decided to take Dollar up on his offer. The funny thing is Dollar said something at night in the car that he was on point about. Love was a good thing, but that hood love was the best kind of love. Although Taylor treating me like a queen, he was too soft for me. I missed riding passenger side in Dollar 's ride while handled his business affairs. The only time Taylor and I were riding was us either going to the movies or yet another restaurant. Our relationship felt like some tour guide type of shit. He seemed more like a tourist than anything else to me. There really wasn't any passion. Don't get me wrong, he was a great guy.

After dealing with Dollar, I swore that I would switch up my taste in men. I did too but honestly, it wasn't working out for me. Now that Dollar was actually back home, those old feelings were starting to resurface. I found myself going back to that whole hood Bonnie lifestyle and shit, no matter what may have happened in the past. No matter how risky that lifestyle had been. No matter how many times I swore I would never go back to the person responsible for introducing me to that kind of Lifestyle. I was addicted to that lifestyle and the man that introduced me to it.

My stomach was now filled with butterflies as I walked around the small closet looking for something to wear. I spotted the outfit that I initially wanted to wear to the club the night of the city's celebration. I picked it up and examined it.

"Nah, this may be a little too granny-ish," I said aloud to no one in particular. "You gotta remind Dollar of what he missed out on!"

"Too granny-ish? I don't think it is. You don't have go out and be dressed like a damn video vixen every day," The sound of my mom's voice made me jump.

"Hey, momma. I didn't know you were standing right there. In fact, I didn't even hear you come home at all."

"I'm sure you didn't. Otherwise, you wouldn't have said what you just did. What's wrong with a nice, comfortable pair of jeans and a nice, t-shirt? See? I've warned you. Always dress the way you want to be approached from this point on. Maybe the next time, you won't be entangled in no hood shit from another damn thug," she fussed per usual. She swore the music I listened to and the way I used to dress back in the day caused me to attract the wrong attention in the first place. That was attention was Dollar.

Rolling my eyes, I tossed the plain jane ass outfit back into the closet bin. My mom was such a vibe killer, it was honestly a shame. Momma was trying her hardest to tighten a leash on me ever since she found out that I almost caught a charge many years ago.

Even though I was now in my mid-20s, she began to treat me as if I was still living in her house or some shit. It had gotten to the point where she wanted to know where I was going, what time I would be back, and who I was going with. It was cool that she was being protective and all. However, that shit went from being protective to overbearing really quick! That's why our bond was weakening instead of strengthening! I think she felt guilty because we didn't always see eye-to-eye when I was growing up.

Although I was the only child, mama really wasn't ready to be a mom at the time. She was still run the streets with her homegirls as if they were twenty-year-olds or something. As a result, I spent most of my free time in the streets as well. I would be walking the different neighborhoods with Jazzy at the time. From what I would see throughout the hood, I knew I wanted to be the wife or girlfriend of a major drug dealer or a hood nigga with major street status. Had my mom sat me down and corrected that kind of behavior early on, I really don't think I would have fallen for Dollar as hard as I did. However, her efforts were too many years and almost a drug trafficking charge too late. Yeah, there were wholesome men out there with good paying jobs and shit. The thing is, a hood nigga with status always made more and could get the pussy ten times wetter.

"Look, ma. I don't know how many times we have to have this conversation, but I will keep telling you this until it's in your head. I am grown. I pay my own bills. You had your turn at raising me. Those first 18 years have now come and gone. Please let me live my life the way I see fit. Even if I was out here selling pussy or slanging dope, it's not your place anymore to tell me what to do and what not to do. You have your opinions just like I have mine, but I don't ask for yours. I know you want what's best for me. But listen, what you may see as best for me is what I may see totally different. That's okay too. You're doing too much for no reason," I explained to her yet again.

"No matter how many bills you pay or how old you turn, you will always be my child. I live with regret everyday knowing that I'm somewhat responsible for your attraction to bad guys. Hell, I liked them too until I finally grew the fuck up and opened my eyes. Falling for these hood dudes with status ain't worth it, baby girl. You would've thought when they threatened you with prison time that you would have left that shit alone for good. You were on the right path until that mothafucka got out and just had to knock you off your game," she fumed, getting visibly upset as if Dollar had me out here potentially facing a murder charge. She was so damn extra, I swear!

"Momma, I swear you are doing way too much right now. Just chill! Let me live my life. I'm good." I leaned over and gave her a quick peck on the cheek. She wiped it off in disgust.

"Girl don't be using those lips on me! Ain't no telling what Dollar 's lips have been on in that damn pen," she joked, but I didn't find it funny one bit. In fact, I was slightly offended. I really didn't know why since it wasn't really my place. Dude had a whole bitch out here, so I don't know why her comment rubbed me the wrong way.

I gave my mom the signature look she had given me plenty of times when I said something stupid. "Really, momma? Please keep the prison stereotypes to yourself because I can assure you that Dollar isn't like that. Besides, he came straight out the joint with some chick."

I didn't even know why I let that slip out of my mouth. My mom was looking at me crazy as hell. Her face was twisted up like a Rubix cube. "And You're proud of that? It seems to me that you're up there bragging about him having someone already. So, you do realize that would make you a side chick, right?"

" mama, we are not dating. How long has it been since I mention Dollar 's name? Years, my point exactly! Therefore, we are not involved with each other. That doesn't mean that we can't be friends or anything like that. After all we do have history. Do I need your permission to have him as a friend now?"

She huffed like a little kid. "Fine! Just don't be surprised when you realize that he's still a piece of shit. I thought you would have learned the first time, but it seems like you didn't. So, I have no other choice but to sit back and watch you find yourself in some deep shit all over again. You may not get lucky this time and be able to get off. Just remember that!"

Not wanting to argue with her because I didn't want her to ruin my vibe, I said, " okay Mama. Did you need anything? I'm not sure as to why you popped up unexpectedly."

"Haha! Now that's real funny. I don't think you've ever tried to put me out of your spot on the sly until now. I need you to get some commonsense ASAP! That's what I need you to do. It's obvious that you're not ready for that right now. I have no other choice but to accept it. Text me when you get home if you aren't feeling yourself too much after this friendship date." without another word she walked out of my room and I heard the front door close to my apartment. I let out a sigh of relief because she was really bugging.

Mentally I had become stronger overtime so I wasn't sure why she thought they Dollar would have me out here doing reckless ass shit. On top of that, I learned my lesson the first time. There wouldn't be a next time. Maybe the chick he was now with would be willing to take the fall for him but not me! If bitches wanted my place from back in the day, then they could definitely have it. Although they wouldn't last a week in my shoes, my position was open. It actually had been open for years now.

Now that she had left, I could get back to concentrating on what I wanted to wear.

Eventually, I settled for a two-piece skirt set with the crop top. Since the clothes didn't need any ironing, I slipped into my clothes and looked at some shoes to wear for the night. I wanted to wear something that would accentuate the muscles in my legs. The thing is, I only had so many heels that Taylor bought me. He loved to purchase me an outfit and shoes for every date night we had. The thing is it seemed like we went out to eat every day, so shoes and outfits were piling up. Eventually I settled for some sandal wedges and called it a day.

I examined myself in a mirror, smiling at what looked back at me. I swear I had the smoothest, brown complexion with big brown eyes. Those restaurants Taylor would take me to had me gaining weight in all the right places, so I had a few extra curves everywhere.

Now that Dollar 's back, it's really time to turn the heat up a bit. I thought to myself as I slipped into the sandal wedges. It's crazy because I swear the chemistry was still there between us two. Anyone could damn near feel it. The only thing is, the timing was no longer right. I'm not sure if it would ever be again. Too much time had passed and there were so many things left unsaid between us.

I applied some light makeup and pinned my hair up. I waited for Dollar 's text, in the meantime, I decided to take two Tums to calm the butterflies that were extremely overly active in my stomach. Being that Dollar was officially back home, I knew it was time for me to boss up. Even if I wanted to remain friends with him, I knew Dollar wouldn't have me out here on some sucker shit!

***

As soon as I got the message that Dollar was outside, I practically ran out of my apartment, nearly falling in the process. I said to hell with double checking myself. Dollar had seen me all dolled up plenty of times before anyways. He knew what was up!

Dollar 's matte black Mercedes G-Wagon truck stood out like a sore thumb over here. Everyone, I included, drove these basic ass cars in my apartment complex. My strides and my smile were much bigger as I headed in the direction of his truck. Usually, I'd be pissed whenever I was in the parking lot of my complex because I would always get harassed by the guys on the basketball court.

With Dollar being back home and people knowing the history we both shared, I knew I wouldn't have to worry about that happening again. The thing is, none of these dudes were on my level around here. I didn't have any more than them financially, but even still, I had so much more to offer. In my eyes, I wasn't some regular chick. My dude needed to have his shit completely together because after Dollar, I swear my standards had become super high. This man had me living the life before he got busted and I ended the relationship. Ultimately, that led to his petty ass having my three months old, baby blue Mercedes Benz being snatched away.

Uh, say Keke, is that you now? Who truck you about to get in?" A voice yelled behind me. I turned around and noticed that it was Demario. Demario was one of the most annoying dudes in our complex. It didn't help that he wanted to be a trapper, so he was always acting like he had it.

Before I could respond, Dollar had rolled down his partially cracked window all the way down. "Yeah, I'm hers. What is it to you, lil nigga?" Dollar inquired with a slightly aggressive tone of voice.

Demario threw his hands up in the air and slowly backed off but before he left, I heard him whisper "he just gon' play yo' ass again" as I opened the door to get in the truck. I don't think he noticed Dollar before Dollar rolled his windows down. Otherwise, he wouldn't had approached me in the first place.

"What did he say to you?" Dollar questioned with a deep frown etched into his face.

"Nothing. If he did, I definitely didn't hear anything," I lied. "I'm always overlooking these people over here." As annoying as Demario was, he didn't deserve to be checked by someone like Dollar. Besides, Dollar hadn't been out a good two weeks yet. He didn't need to take any chances of going back especially over something so petty and so minor. However, it did sting a bit knowing that everyone was basically calling me stupid for entertaining Dollar again. This just goes to show that everyone knew what went down between us. Lowkey, I was now salty and didn't really want to be seen out with him.

He turned to me and slightly frowned up even harder. "Keke! What the fuck is that shit on your face?"

"It's makeup by MAC, duh, " I stammered over my words as he caught me off guard.

"I don't give a damn if it's makeup by Sephora or that damn Rihanna, you don't need to be wearing that shit. You already look good as hell. Now I really won't be able to get all these niggas off you! On a more serious note, you know you don't need anything to enhance your beauty but some Vaseline here and there when your lips get dry. That's it. You look ten years older with that shit on your face. You used to cry about me making you act older than you actually wore. Now look at you! Walking around here like you just grown-grown and shit!"

I finally found my voice which is something I had to do right now. Otherwise, this night would consist of Dollar feeling as if he could say what the fuck he wanted without any consequences. I couldn't have that. Besides, I wasn't his girl, so it wasn't his place to complain about what I wore and didn't wear.

Listen you doing too much right about now. You asked me to come on his friendship date and I did. You didn't mention any other requirements. Even if you did, I still wouldn't have followed. Remember we are friends and nothing more. I don't move when you tell me to move. I don't apply or not apply makeup when you want me to. I am not your new girl or your do girl. Let's get that straight right now and right before we get too far away from my place. If you think you can get through dinner without criticizing me then let's go to dinner. If not, then it's not too late to turn around and take me back home."

Dollar glared at me before taking an incoming call on his phone. Though the volume was up, I couldn't quite make out what the person was saying on the other end.

"Fuck, fuck!" He cursed out loud. "I'll be on my way in a minute. Say KEKE, something just came up. I need to handle some business right quick. Do you want me to take you back home or are you fine with coming along?"

"Nah, I'm good. Remember who you currently have sitting passenger side. I'm not new to this shit. I'm true to it. Let's ride!"

"Cool, cool! Part of me figured you would be down. The other half wasn't so sure since you seem like a changed woman and shit! FYI though, you will not be getting out. Imma go inside and take care of some business. Then I'm coming back out. I'm not trying to get you caught up like last time. I learned my lesson. On another note though, who was dude back there in yo' complex?" he continued to inquire. Though I would never call him out on it, he definitely was jealous right now and I loved every bit of that shit.

"Demario? Tuh! That man could never get a chance although he keeps begging for one. For one, he isn't my type. For two, dude is nothing but a lazy ass bum. Nah, I'm good."

"Shit, I bet his swagger is better than ol' boy you are messing with now. From what I'm hearing, you got yo' self a lil' college boy. Graduated from Tulane? Engineering major guy?" he asked. "You don't even have to answer because I already know."

"Why are you so inquisitive? Damn! You traded becoming a kingpin to a damn cyberstalker when you were behind bars, I see. All of that information is correct. Whoever is your source, I hope you've compensated them well. They are definitely on point," I admitted. There was no need in lying because he pretty much knew everything already. Besides, nothing about Taylor would cause me to be embarrassed of him.

He reminded me of Dollar Tate, I swear. The only difference is, Taylor was a bit of a nerd compared to him. How did I end up going from a kingpin to a damn nerd? I don't know! But you better believe that my mom approved of him even if I necessarily didn't…well now I didn't. Now that I was back in Dollar 's presence.

"I mean you know we would have to do some catching up eventually. You're being sensitive as hell. Loosen up! Relax! You are more than welcome to ask me the same questions I'm asking you. I'm a grown ass man with nothing to hide. You're grown too, but you're dancing around the questions as if you're ashamed of your dude. If you love him, then don't be afraid to claim him. Fuck what I think, right? I mean, it was fuck me after I got hit with my sentence. So, I'm not sure why you're trying to protect my feelings, if that's what you call yourself doing," he called me out.

I ignored Dollar the entire drive to wherever we were going. His remarks were way too smart for me.

Dollar parked his truck once we pulled up in front of a decent sized house that was surrounded by rundown houses with overgrown grass in the front. There were several people roaming the block from bums to guys who were dressed up like gangsters. My body immediately realized. Although I hadn't been on this side of town, I knew that if mothafuckas respected Dollar, then he would make sure that they respected me too. I tugged on my seatbelt, preparing to get out. That's when I felt Dollar touch my thigh, making my insides tingle a bit at his touch.

"Chill, shorty. I can tell you're excited over there, but I wasn't playing. Your ass is not coming inside. Cause if some shit goes down, I don't even have to worry about what will happen to you in the process. It's gon' be harder to clear your name if you're placed at the scene again. Just chill! I got this," he said so smoothly.

"Chill? In the hood of all places? This is like my neck of the woods in a way. Let me see what's going on or something. How can you bring me along but make me sit in the car? Huh?"

He chuckled. "Baby girl, we not about to do this. Before I let you come inside, I will take your ass all the way back home and just drive back over here once I drop you off."

"And that would be doing way too much to try to prove a point. Take you back home if you want to. I bet I get in my car and come right back over here. Try me," I challenged him. "It's too late to treat me like a rookie now. You had me doing your dirty work right alongside you. Don't act like I'm not capable of doing it now. See you starting to soften up on me. I guess that chick is getting inside your head after all. Just because you can't take care of two every hood, it does not mean that it applies to me! Now let's go," I demanded, finally putting my foot down with him!

He chuckled again while massaging my thigh. "Damn baby girl! As much as I don't want you to come inside, the way you just put your foot down got my dick hard as fuck right about now. Why couldn't you just stay down? Damn it, Keke! A nigga wanna be mad at you so damn right now, but you just made me say fuck dismissing me once I got locked up. C'mon!"

"You did me wrong, I did you wrong," I started.

"You take me back, I take you back," he sang, causing me to bend over in laughter. "Ain't that what Pleasure P said in that song?"

Playfully, I mushed his head. "Hell yeah! That used to be our song too, huh? Back in the good ol' days, but don't try to pull out that lyric right now! That song does NOT apply to this situation right now."

"Okay, I'mma chill before you go ghost on my ass again. I meant to ask you, what do you do for a living now?"

""Oh, so you mean to tell me that your little spies I didn't tell you that either? That person was slipping then! It was hard trying to find a job after that incident between us, so I had to do what you told me how to do. You told and taught me how to hustle at an early age, so I applied that shit later on in life too. Right now, I'm running my own online boutique. It's not as much cash as it used to be from back in the day, but it's consistent. It keeps the lights on, and the rest of my bills paid." My business may have had more downs than ups compared to the Dollar 's drug business but I will say that I applied the things I learned from him into my business!

"So basically, I'm about to continue selling dope and shit, while you sell your hair bundles and lashes on the side right. Did I get it right?" Dollar smiled, exposing the whitest set of teeth I had ever seen for him to have been incarcerated.

"You're working overtime right now to get back on my good side but keep on thinking that. I never said I was going to give you another chance. That's your problem now! You're so damn cocky and used to getting what you want."

"Evidently not! Part of me still wants you and you keep shooting a nigga down. So, do I really have what I want?"

"Well, let's not get technical here. Business only, period!"

Without another word, we both got out of the truck. Shit, it was my first time here and I felt like I owned this spot and the block. In fact, I began walking before Dollar could come from around his truck. I was mid-stride when I felt Dollar pull me back.

"I don't know what the fuck you're on right now, but you need to chill. What if I was going to meet with an enemy and you're walking ahead of me like you just run shit? Huh?" He asked with an attitude.

I pushed his hand away since he had a light grip on me in the first place. Sucking my teeth, I said, "Really Dollar? When have you ever been known to meet up with enemies? You're the most respected and most feared dude in all of New Orleans. Just face it! You're feeling some type of way because I'm not scared. I'm still that bossed up ass bitch from back in the day. You know this!" I said, flipping my long weave in the process. I knew I was putting Dollar 's new chick to shame right about now. Crazy thing is, I wasn't even acting or trying too hard. Being in this particular setting while standing next to Dollar, naturally brought the old Keke back to life.

Finally, we went inside of Dollar 's new trap house. I must admit, this was the modern version of what we used to operate out of back in the day. The one back then, you could literally ride by and take a guess of what would be going on in the inside just from looking outside. However, this one looked like a single-family home. The very front of the house looked like a well-decorated living room. Nothing looked out of the ordinary until we headed to the back. There was a huge room that reminded me of a science lab exhibit. There were a group of huge, buff men standing around. Some faces I recognized from back in the day, some were new faces or new recruits.

"I don' told y'all niggas about eating that phony ass Cajun from around the block," Dollar yelled, getting straight into boss mode. "Y'all niggas are free to go home. I expect y'all mothafuckas to be back here bright and early tomorrow. We got too much product that needs to be out on our streets. What's the point of having all these bitches and parading them around the city that can't even feed y'all before coming to work? That's why y'all need to get some bitches who knows how to do more than riding and sucking dick, then y'all asses won't have to worry about food poisoning. I've been gone way too long. Now that I'm back and ready to work, y'all nigga wanna play. Hell nah!" he continued to fuss.

Some people tried to laugh, but I could see the pained expressions on their faces as they grabbed their keys and other things to leave. Once everyone left, it was just Dollar and me alone. If I had some sleeves on, I would've rolled them mothafuckas up. I knew what time it was! Dollar didn't have to utter a word.

"Should I go make sure the front door is locked? I mean, this is a new spot and all, but you know how these Feds be! We don't need nobody tryna run up in here," I told him.

"Relax, baby girl. I'll protect you from whatever's going on outside of that door. But nah, you don't have to. Like I said, I'm a little wiser and less cocky now. I have a few soldiers all around this block for any potential enemies. As far as the feds go, I think they may be able to turn a blind eye now. I'm paying my lawyer and them quite well to cooperate together accordingly."

He immediately pulled out a switch blade and started tearing boxes open. I looked around until I saw another spare box cutter that was left lying around. He didn't have to ask me or tell me what to do, I already knew what to do. I cut across the brown material. I already knew it was cocaine inside the boxes. It had to be as it had always been Dollar 's bestselling products. These were the bricks the rap stars referred to in the rap songs. I swear I got an adrenaline rush just doing this all over again. This felt better than when the packs came in from my clothing vendors.

"This is your first time seeing this in a long time, right?" Dollar asked.

"You already know it is," I admitted. "This sure isn't Taylor's lane!"

"I need to break all of this down by tomorrow tonight. You think you can help me out since my help is sick? I hate I'm even asking you this, but I really don't have anyone else right now."

Although I said I was done with that lifestyle, I figured why not. It's the least I could do since I knew he really didn't have any other assistance.

I shrugged. "Yeah, I'm cool with it. One thing though, don't think that this is my way of approving what you did to me many years ago. I'm just stepping in as a friend. I mean, you need to teach your girl how to do this too or something. This is my first and last time helping."

"I promise I won't ask you again. Like I said, I feel bad for having to ask in the first place. If it makes you feel better, then just know that I would never purposely set you up. That's why I worked hard so that you could get your freedom."

I watched as Dollar pulled out a few bricks. He placed two in front of him and two in front of me.

"The first thing you want to do is take the knife next to you and cut a fine, thin line. Next place it in a baggie, press it down with the grinder until it breaks," he instructed as if this was my first time doing this. I watched as he cut one brick extremely fast. All of a sudden, I got nervous just thinking about whether I could still do this shit or not. It had been so long.

He must've noticed my hands trembling as I started to cut because he said, "Damn, Keke. I guess you really weren't lying. Let me show you everything again. I'm not mad or anything like that. In fact, I'm happy. It goes to show you weren't out here chasing after every nigga that claimed to sell drugs and shit!"

I laughed, which surprisingly caused me to relax a whole lot. "Boy, I was not thinking about no other drug dealers at the time. I was trying to get my life back together."

"Well, let me help you get your life back together," he offered.
I didn't know what he really meant so I said, "Oh, is that right?"

He stepped closer to me. In fact, we were so close to each other, I'm sure we could smell each other's breath.

"I'm serious, Shawty. I know since I've been home that you've been reconsidering everything. I don't see you and ol' boy lasting much longer now that I'm back. You should come fuck with a real nigga again."

I didn't want to be stupid for Dollar, but I also knew that there was some truth to what he was saying. I really didn't see Taylor and I lasting much longer. Unfortunately, Taylor was a good ass dude, but he wasn't of my speed. Sometimes women could really be too much for men and that was true in my relationship right now. I was definitely too much for Taylor. Now that Dollar was out, I had been thinking hard about our future. Well, if there could ever be a future with us again.

"Dollar, I don't like how you keep making it seem like I'm the only one right now with someone. I haven't told you Taylor's life story, but I also haven't denied him either. I think you're forgetting that I know about that chick whose texts you read out loud. You keep telling me to drop Taylor when you're not even trying to drop your bitch. No sir, this will not go your way. You're not about to have me out here sharing you."

He shook my body lightly. "Calm down, Keke. I never said anything about becoming official right now. I just got out a long ass sentence. I need time to sit down and think first. I know who my soulmate is. Do I know if soulmates are meant to be together again? No, not yet! I want us to take things slow. Did I say you need to go home and cut Taylor off at this very moment? Nah! I can't fault you for moving on. We both thought I would be serving a life sentence. You held me down and I appreciate that shit. I wasn't expecting you to marry a nigga behind bars or even stay with me, so that's definitely not the case.

Of course, I was slightly jealous to know that you moved on. However, I understand all that shit. As far as me and Misha go, I know that I don't want her ass. She's just something to do when there was nothing to do. Now that I'm out, it's back to work. I'm only focusing on what really matters at the moment. So, can I at least take you to dinner another time?"

"If the date involves eating food and not spending time in your trap house, then yeah. I'm trying to stay on the right path. Momma so damn paranoid, she acts like I'm about to throw my life away because I tagged along with you."

He licked his sexy, plump lips. "Bet that up! And yo' momma has never been fond of me. I can't blame her though. I would be overprotective of my daughter too. It's cool. She can hate that you're hanging with me but she better know that I'll put my life on the line for you without hesitation. Yeah, we may package a few drugs here and there, but I swear you're safe with me. You've always been safe with me," he said.

I examined my work while nodding my head. I was such a perfectionist, which is funny because I was doing something so illegal. At the same time, it felt good as hell. Dollar was geeked as fuck too. I could tell by the grin he kept trying so hard to mask.

"So, who is responsible for all of this if you said you're gonna take the backseat?" I inquired curiously.

"My last task is breaking it down and bagging it up. You and me just need to let it sit so that it can dry. After that, I will let them distribute. No more doing the dirty work, you feel me? That's when shit goes south."

I knew I was asking for a bit too much, but I decided to ask anyway. "Do you ever think we can take over New Orleans like we were on the path to doing back then?"

He laughed. "After this, it's all out of my hands for good. I no longer believe in getting my hands dirty. It's a vow I made to my granny and my lawyer once I stepped off that old ass property. My lawyer made a point. That's why I have an entire loyal team to do this for me in case of risks...you know? Matter of fact, this shit is lowkey hitting me differently since it's been so long that I've been around it. I just had to step in since they got sick. Let me find out you're slowly wanting to get back into this shit, lowkey."

"Actually, I kind of am. I swear it's nothing like that fast money. Shit is moving too slow in my life and my drug dealing skills are impeccable. I can't be around here shaking no ass for no petty ass cash either. Bitches just don't know that the drug game is where it's at. Period!"

"If Mama was about to have a heart attack about me dealing drugs then imagine how she would flip if she found out that I was stripping or into sex work or some chick." Just hearing my mom inside my head right now made me tremble. I knew that was one thing that she wouldn't let me live down."

"Hell yeah! You already know that, but truth be told I would much rather you deal drugs than shake your ass. There are too many predators out there. At least with you being in a male-dominated game people would hesitate to try you. Especially because they know that we are affiliated in one way or another. I don't think they would try you at the strip club either but there's some risk I wouldn't want to take. Even if we aren't together and even if we don't get back together, your safety will forever be my top priority."

"Thank you, Dollar! And just like I prayed for you day in and day out despite us not talking. Like you said whether we're together or not, I always got you! You definitely brought me out of some hard times back in the day. You taught me how to hustle which I didn't know I would still need years later but hey! We're good."

"What do you think about your mama? I was just thinking that since my business life is about to slow down that it may be time to actually settle down. I feel like you're my soulmate. As crazy as it sounds and considering our circumstances, I know this! I actually feel this with every fiber in my bone. I just don't have time for the lack of support from family members. Eventually what people say about a person to you will have some effect on you. Believe it or not!"

"Oh, I most definitely agree! I think people are still judging me based on what happened between us in the past. At first, they didn't bother me but then I sat back and was like, did I really make a fool out of myself? No did I let you make a fool out of me! I thought I was on some ride or die type of shit, but people got me convinced that I'm just on some stupid and dumb shit," I finally confessed to him.

"First off who is people? Give me some names and location so that I can go talk to them! Did any of those people put you in a better position than I did back then? Did I hold a gun up to your head and forced you to partake in any of my illegal activities? Did they help you out the struggle back then? And for your mama to be up there talking, she knows that she also benefited. I hope she don't think that you were working a legal job while managing to pay her bills too. C'mon now! Since when did you start listening to what people have to say? I couldn't even get you to listen to me when I told your ass not to get out that truck! So now all of a sudden, you're listening to people? Interesting!"

"It's mostly my mom pointing out how stupid I was! Please don't go wreaking havoc in these streets over some nonsense. I can see that stupid look you have in your eyes. Dollar, you are still on that same shit and I can't tolerate that! You know my mom has no filter when it comes to any and everything."

"See? That's where I have to stop you. It's not about what she says to you, it's all about what you allow her to say to you. You have to put a stop to her. You're grown as hell out here. So, if she's skeptical about you being around me, then why are you around me now? I'm not trying to have her ass be the one to blow up my spot just to prove a point!"

"That's the thing, she knows we're out together. I told her that we were going on a friendship date. Like grabbing ice cream or some shit. She doesn't know that we're at a traphouse." My lips quivered a bit because I was so nervous talking to Dollar.

"What the fuck? What does it look like my overgrown ass taking you out to get some ice cream? You got me fucked up and I'm not Taylor! That shit would be more convincible if you were out and about with him. Even still, nah shorty it doesn't work like that with me.

This shit seems like you're embarrassed by me or something when I did nothing but put your ass in a position to win. Not only that, what if I actually wanted more with you, Keke? You would have to lie about your whereabouts or have your people in your ear feeding you poisonous shit about me. I'm too grown for the bullshit. I need my woman to be grown too. I can't be out here dating someone, and their people don't approve of me. I can't guarantee that I'll have the patience for all that nonsense talk. You know what? Forget all that shit! Let me go ahead and take you home before your phone starts ringing off the hook. I don't have time for nobody's momma to be talking out the side of their neck. My grandma old as hell, but she will defend the fuck out of me if need be too," he huffed.

I noticed Dollar had flipped the switch on me really quick after my comments clearly rubbed him the wrong way. I didn't want to further upset him, so I snatched my purse off the big packaged box and began to walk out of the workroom.

"Look at ya! Carrying that granny ass purse that ya momma probably picked out for you like she did your boyfriend," Dollar mumbled underneath his breath, but I still heard him. Instead of responding, I kept walking trying my hardest to contain my laughter. Dude was pressed as hell right now.

As soon as I made it to his truck and was about to tug on the handle to get in, he purposely locked it with the remote. As upset and bothered as I was, I pretended not to be. I couldn't give his ass the satisfaction that he so desperately wanted.

Although there were a few bums who looked like they were coming in my direction, I shrugged all that shit off. I texted Jazzy to see what she had planned, and she told me to come through so that we could chat. Finally, Dollar walked out with a frown on his face. I didn't get why he was so upset. I never said that it was time for me to go home and even my momma overbearing ass couldn't force me to go home. The car ride back to my place was silent between the both of us. The only thing that could be heard is the navigation system instructing how to get to my apartment. That's all. Finally, Dollar pulled up to my complex.

I hopped out the truck. "Bye."

"Tell your momma that I brought you back from your ice cream date while it was still daylight out, so she should be good. We didn't get into no drivebys or no shit like that," he spat just before speeding out of the complex, blasting his loud ass music. I couldn't do anything but shake my head as I headed to my two-year-old Honda Accord.

I started the car and sat there for a minute. It was too damn hot inside my car to be trying to drive right now. I looked to the side and spotted Demario running towards my car.

Ugh! Where is Dollar when you need him? What the hell does he want now? I thought to myself.

I know it hadn't been long since I left with Dollar, but damn! Demario still had on his dingy, off-white muscle shirt that clung to his extra sweaty body. He had on the same sagging basketball shorts that showed his dirty ass Hanes drawers. With this Louisiana heat, I'm sure his entire body reeked of funk and smelled like total ass!

"What do you want, Demario?" I asked in an agitated tone of voice. I had been here for almost a year now and he still hadn't learned that I wasn't interested in him. It seemed like the more I pushed him away, the more he tried to gravitate towards me. Eventually, I was bound to snap on his ass.

He wiped his face using his shirt. The off-white shirt had become even filthier. It was covered in brown dirt from his skin. I shuddered at the sight. I swear I wanted to dump some dishwashing liquid and a bucket of water on his ass right about now.

"Why do you have an attitude? If anything, I should be the one with the attitude. Since when did you and Dollar get back together? And I thought you had a man. The one that drives the white boy SUV," he asked nosily with no shame at all.

My nostrils were now flared because he had his hairy ass armpit on top of my car. Between my air running and the slight breeze, I could literally smell his funky odor.

I held my breath while trying to respond. "Stay the fuck out of my business, Demario. Although I'm deeply concerned about you, you don't see me in your damn business!"

"Nah, cause that's some foul shit right there, 'Keke. You claimed you didn't want to give me the time of day because of my lifestyle and look at you now. Does it look like your taste in men has truly changed? You could've given me the time of day. At least I wouldn't be stupid enough to have you doing my dirty work. I can't say the same for ol' boy though. And you let that nigga back in so damn easily. What makes you think he won't try you again? You really the most loyal chick I know throughout the city. I like that shit though. I hate that you're loyal to the wrong person though. You're a good girl and I already know you got some good pussy. At least be with a man that's good for you in every aspect of your life. I can be the best nigga you ever had," He practically shouted that last part.

"And you got some sweaty, stinky balls. I can smell them now. Move before I tase the hell out of you. How can you do shit for me when you can't even wash your own ass properly? Boy bye! This will be the only time of day you get from me. The next time you wanna speak on Dollar, then walk your ass to his truck and get it off your chest. You should be thanking me because I definitely spared you earlier." I threw my car in drive, then sped off. One thing was for sure, I had grown tired of my past being brought up in every conversation. It was as if the entire New Orleans would never let me live that down. The crazy thing is, I think people really thought Dollar set me up. Yeah, I was doing his dirty work right beside him. The thing is, the Feds came and raided his spot. They were out here thinking this man would literally get me caught up in some shit. Not Dollar! He was the most solid dude ever!

**

"Hey bestfrandddd," Jazzy sang a bit dryly. Jazzy was sprawled out on her queen-sized bed with her phone in her hand.

I got comfortable on the bed. "Uhh, what's wrong with you?"

She sat up and started talking. "You remember the guy I left with at Dollar 's party, right?"

"How could I forget? You left me with Dollar because of Draco's ugly ass!"

She playfully slapped me upside the head with the pillow. "Oh, shut up, hell. Anyway, he was supposed to take me out on a date last week, right? Girl, I had gotten dressed and everything. I had on my 'fuck me' thong just in case some shit was bound to go down since our HIV tests came back negative, but you know we were gonna strap up either way it goes. No glove, no love from me! I even did my infamous vinegar and lavender oil soak. I doubled up on my dosage of probiotics too, just in case, he wanted to put his face down there. Shit, none of that happened. I mean none of it!"

"My first question is this, how did all of this happen without Tanya knowing? You know she's so damn clingy and overprotective. Nothing gets past her and I do mean nothing!"

Tanya and I bumped heads a lot when Jazzy and Tanya started dating. I came in the picture before her, but she tried to get rid of me. If that made any sense. She thought I was a member of the Pretty Kitty Bandit, as Jazzy called it when that wasn't the case at all. Despite Jazzy's preference, she never looked at me in a sexual way. We were two best friends who could sleep in the same bed together and I never had to worry about her touching me in an unwanted manner. Tanya couldn't seem to grasp that, so she spent time trying to break up our friendship. However, she eventually learned that I wasn't going anywhere, and she got in formation really quick.

She rolled her eyes up at the ceiling. "Chile, I broke up with Tanya. Well, she actually broke up with me, but you know I had been waiting for this day for a minute now. She basically said that I wasn't the only one, which is fine by me. I've been craving some real, masculine dick for a minute now," she laughed. "Not that rubbery silicone shit! I wanted that real thang, baby!"

"Well, you know what that song said! I keep telling y'all, y'all need a reality show or a YouTube with the entertainment y'all provide. Anyway, what did Draco say about canceling y'all plans last minute?"

"He said something came up, but I know better than to believe that. A fine man like Draco has tons of options, I already know. His favorite hoe probably called him on some freaky shit, so he bailed out on me. You know that nigga was fresh out of the pen too. He probably had to go fuck them bitches that were visiting or writing him."

She said it without any emotions whatsoever. For the life of me, I didn't understand how Jazzy could settle for crap like that.

"And um, you're okay with that?"

"Am I okay with him having options? Yeah, I'm okay with it for now. We aren't together. We're just vibing. I have to earn being a priority in his life just like he has to earn becoming one in mine. But what's up with you and Dollar? And I see you got this damn basic outfit on you was so desperate to wear to the club," she giggled. "I'm so glad you didn't wear this one!"

I examined my outfit. It did become even more casual looking the longer I looked at it. It wasn't something you would wear to a poppin' ass club. "I just actually left from hanging with Dollar --"

"Oh no you didn't bitch," she gasped. "Why didn't you tell me? So, how's the jail dick? I heard that sex when a dude first gets out is the best sex ever. I mean, if y'all got that far. I'm skeptical of dudes who've been in there awhile. Did he ask for anal sex? That's usually a sign. I need to know what Draco may hit me with so that I can be prepared."

"I was going to tell you all that before your ass interrupted me. Anyway, I actually wanted to look cute for him, but you know how my mom feels about Dollar. She popped up at random. I swear it's like she damn near sensed that I would be going out with him or something. I told her though. Girl, did she get upset! She started nagging and telling me to basically stop being so damn stupid for Dollar. You know she's Team Taylor, but I truly think it's out of guilt. I think she's feeling guilty because she was in and out of the house when she should've been raising me. Anyway, I'm not sure what Dollar had planned for us because we didn't get to do anything other than going to his new trap house."

"I don't mean to keep interrupting you, but you went where? To the damn trap house?" She shouted, which was okay because I was at her place, safe from my momma's ears. "Aww shit, here we go again. Hood Clyde strikes again!"

"Girl, yes! His guys got sick from eating some damn Cajun food, so we went to his new traphouse. Girl, I didn't even know the man had a new traphouse. Of course, I rolled up my invisible sleeves and got to work."

"No ma'am! Get the hell out, bitch! I can't believe you lied about putting that kind of lifestyle behind you." She constantly shook her head.

"I was serious at the time, Jazzy. I actually loved doing it although Dollar did have to reteach me all the steps. Girl, listen! With this economy changing rapidly and me having bills to pay, I can't be out here missing out on some money," I laughed. "Slow money is usually legal money while fast money isn't. Bills come in just as quickly as they go out. I'm sorry but shit, I got to eat, period! My mom may hate Dollar 's guts, but I don't. Like he said, he put me and my mom in a position to win. We all know that I took care of my mom off Dollar 's bread when we were together."

"Yes! That's true which is why I wish she wouldn't talk down on him. It's sad either way it goes. I knew you still cared about Dollar, but your mom is known to hold a grudge. I feel like entertaining him would cause you to lose the bond you're now building with her. Also, you would probably lose Dollar too since they both don't have a filter and would tell each other off every change they get. I keep telling you, you need to put her in her place. If she can't accept that you're grown and can date whoever you want despite their occupation, then she needs to find a man she can control herself. You're no longer at the age where you can be controlled."

I agreed with her. "Yeah, that's exactly why I'm over here now. Dollar said the same thing in so many words. He was actually upset and saying things such as he brought me home from our ice cream date while there was still some sunlight out. Now he knows damn well that I live by myself."

"Damn Shawty," she giggled. "An ice cream date of all places? I'm getting secondhand embarrassment from just listening. My parents knew once they moved me into my dorm first year of college that they could no longer control my life. Yeah, they had opinions and what not, but they knew theirs didn't count. I'll listen because that's why I got ears, but that doesn't mean I'm obligated to take your advice."

I laid back on the bed and checked to see if I had any messages. Particularly a message from Dollar, but there wasn't one. My messages were full of people asking me to restock certain clothing items, which was my main income for the time being.

"It is embarrassing, which is why I plan on talking to my mother. I gotta get it through her head one good time that I am not tolerating her foolishness. Whatever opinions she has about Dollar, then she needs to keep them to herself. I'm sick of people acting like this man had bad intentions when he didn't."

Jazzy looked at me in disbelief. "When, girl? You've been saying that for the longest now. I still feel like she forced you to like Taylor.

She forced you so much that you ended up liking him a bit. Deep down inside, you know you want a hood nigga. See, I'm understanding because I'm a girl, I'm your friend. However, a nigga doesn't understand why you're letting your mom make these decisions in your life. Especially at your age. You're grown as hell; Dollar is grown as hell. What makes you think he's about to actually date a girl who feels like she needs her mom's full approval of the guy?"

As right as Jazzy was, I hated how these conversations turned into personal attacks sort of. I wasn't about to talk to my mom crazy the way Jazzy had a tendency of doing growing up. Hell nah! My mom was waaaay younger than her parents, so she wasn't with the shits. She still had the strength to knock me off my ass if she ever wanted to.

"Well, this may be a sign that I don't need to get involved with him again. I've been getting nothing but backlash whenever his name is mentioned," I said sadly.

"Unfortunately, it just may be. It's sad that you didn't get a chance to pop that pussy for a real nigga again. I remember you complaining about Taylor in bed at some point."

I shook my head at Jazzy while laughing. The bitch didn't forget a damn thing you said to her. She would always bring them up at the most inconvenient times too. I was left wondering though. Dollar said that I was his soulmate. I felt the same thing too, but what if soulmates weren't actually meant to be together? Damn!

***

CHAPTER SIX:
DOLLAR TATE
KEKE vs. THEM

My unexpected hood date had been going so perfect with Keke until she just had to bring up these speculators' opinions about me. I could understand if these people were genuinely concerned about her well-being, but they had no reason to be out here acting like I had shorty out here prostituting or some shit like that. From my understanding, Keke and her mom were supposed to be strengthening their bond. Yet, why did her mom choose to bond over me? I was a grown ass man, so I needed a fully-grown ass woman. I confided in my grandma too but damn, there were certain things she couldn't tell me. Honestly, that's why I was more upset than anything. I had too many grown bitches to ever settle for messing with someone who had people around that didn't approve of my lifestyle.

Still frustrated, I headed to Naudia's place. Naudia was second in line compared to Misha. As much as I would've preferred Misha's mouth and its services over Naudia's, Misha's mouth is exactly why she was on punishment right now. She had the nerve to call me earlier this week, questioning me and my whereabouts. That was a big no-no in my book. So, until further notice, I wasn't fucking with her. She couldn't keep up with a nigga now that I was out of them shackles and it was fucking with her.

I called Naudia up and she answered damn near on the last ring as if she had a point to prove. Although she and Misha weren't my only hoes, they were my top two. It was crazy how opposite they were. Misha would drop everything and answer my call on the first ring, whereas, Naudia would wait until the call dang near went to voicemail. Naudia acted as if she didn't need me, but Misha most definitely did. One thing was for sure, they both had something in common and that is their love for what I toted in my jeans. I mean, it's not like they were getting the heart that was under my shirt.

"Open up the damn door, girl," I demanded just before ending the call.

"Um, I swear I didn't know you were coming over." She started picking things up around the living room. The living room wasn't exactly a mess, but it wasn't clean either. As long as she didn't have roaches running across the room, then I was good. That's how you knew when a chick was really trifling and dirty.

Chicks don't want me to see how they're really living. I thought to myself.

I turned around if I was about to leave. "Aw, I didn't know I had to alert you. I guess I'll leave then."

As expected, Naudia begged for me to stay while tugging on my new GUCCI shirt.

"You know I was just talking, baby! You can pop up on me anytime." She went into the small kitchen to throw away the small trash in her hand and when she returned, she said, "I need to go hop in the shower really quick. It will be quick, I promise!"

"Aye! I mean, do what you gotta do to make sure I don't get no sweaty, hair, funky pussy."

She quickly scurried off to the bathroom, which had me fucking dying on the inside. See, I had always let my chicks know when I was coming through before I got locked up. There would always be like an hour gap or so in between time, so it gave them time to wash up and all that good stuff. My motto with anything in life was this simple ass saying, "if you stay ready, then you don't have to get ready." Pussy was also included in that motto, but I swear chicks acted as if they didn't understand. Knowing Naudia, she was probably in the bathroom about to tear the damn door off the hinges trying to get to her razor, shaving cream and some Summer's Eve body wash. When in reality, these chicks needed to stay up to date on their intake of probiotics and stay hydrated with water and fruits and watch the number of different dicks they were taking. That's all.

I swear almost forty minutes had gone by and I could still hear her water running from the bathroom. So, I went to see what the hell was going on. If she really had this deep care routine, she had to perform just to receive the dick, then that usually indicated that there was a major problem that was usually being masked. It wasn't like I was going to bless her with some head or anything like that though.

"SAY," I called out. "Girl, if the water hasn't done its change then I'm sure it won't. I'm sure that water has turned cold by now."

She didn't respond, instead, she finally shut the water off. I swear, this was the type of shit that would make it hard for me to get on hard. If this is what all chicks had to do before I came over, then I definitely didn't want to know. Shit, I would've started coming over two hours later just to avoid this.

Naudia returned to the living room with just a towel wrapped around her body while sporting a big grin. Her ass damn sure didn't have that same energy a few minutes ago when I popped up on her.

"I just gotta know forreal. What in the hell took you so damn long?" I was now annoyed as hell and unable to mask my deep frustration.

"Don't worry about all that. Just sit back and enjoy what's next to come," Naudia dropped the towel, exposing her naked body.

She had a few stretch marks on her titties that now had fresh tiger paw tats on them which I hadn't seen in a hot ass minute. Having two kids, who now lived with their fathers, had done her body some justice. I didn't like to compare Keke to these hoes, but she had perky breasts and a fat ass that I loved to grab on when I would hit it from the back. Naudia went for my Louis Vuitton belt buckle and then unzipped my pants where I was sort of already waiting in anticipation. Shit, the foreplay was really waiting on her ass to finally get out the shower. She dropped down to her knees and placed her wet mouth on my dick. The noticeable color contrast definitely made me even harder. I was dark and she was a lil' light bright. I could tell that she had tightened up on her mouth skills because she was using fewer teeth and more spit from the few times she would come visit me in the joint. There was no telling who taught her how to do tricks with her mouth but it sure wasn't me. I didn't like to teach women when it came to sexual fulfillment and things like that. We were at the age where we should've known how to please each other's bodies by now. If you didn't have it then you just didn't have it!

"Shitttt, Naudia," I moaned through gritted teeth as she continued to bob her head up and down. She continued to do so until my seeds shot down in her throat. Or at least that's what I thought occurred.

Shawty opened her mouth and literally poured the stringy nut onto her fingers. She had the nerve to place her fingers near her pussy as if she was about to stick the cum up her freshly shaved pussy. Why did she do that?

WHAP!

The sound of my hand landing across the side of Naudia's face bounced off the walls. The mixture of both the saliva and cum had hit the floor.

"Hoe, don't you ever in your life try to pull some trifling ass shit like that. Don't ever try to sit up and make a baby that I'm not willing to give your ass. Just for that shit, I'm done fucking with you real shit," I snapped. "You got the nerve to try to stuff some shit up your pussy when you need to find out what needs to come out of it. Don't forget yo' ass stayed in the shower for almost an hour!"

Naudia stared at me in disbelief and horror as tears streamed down her face. "I'm gonna leave yo' crazy, felonious ass alone," she shouted.

I laughed. "That's cool, shorty. It's already been established that I'm done fucking with you. And another thing, I don't get left by bitches, I'm the one that leaves bitches."

I readjusted my pants and left Naudia's lil spot. I couldn't believe shorty tried to trap me right in front of my eyes without giving a damn about the potential consequences. She was definitely bold as hell. None of it made sense to me, though. Why would she want to trap me with a kid when she had two that already didn't even live with her? Maybe it was a sign that I needed to settle down and stick to one chick only. I should've taken my ass home after tonight's crazy ass scare, but there was one person I wanted to see right now…

10:10 P.M.

After putting Keke's new address in my navigation system, I headed to her apartment complex. I realized that I definitely overreacted earlier and wanted to apologize without actually saying "I'm sorry" because those were two words that would never come out of my mouth. I didn't even apologize to the judge when he claimed that I was ruining so many lives in New Orleans with my high-grade drug supply. About thirty minutes later, I pulled up. As expected, she was now at home. Was it really a coincidence that she was home at this time of night? I didn't think so. I couldn't do anything but laugh as I dialed her up. This was our first time ever talking on the phone since I had been released, so I hoped she would answer. Hell, she barely answered my fed calls. Now I realized that her mom definitely had a role in all that.

"Dollar," she answered, which really shocked the living hell out of me.

"Say, I need to talk to you for a quick. Aye, come out and holla at ya' boy!"

"But -," she started.

"But nothing. Just bring your lil' ass outside like I said. I'm pretty sure you aren't tied up right now."

"Ugh, okay. Here I come," she huffed like a little kid.

"Cool! And one last thing," I called out.

"What is that thing, Dollar?"

"If you have to call up your mom and tell her that you're going outside to talk to me, then don't please bother coming out." I disconnected the call and waited for Keke to come on out. She came downstairs in a bonnet, a pair of Victoria's Secret PJ's and some fuzzy ass slippers. I swear Keke looked good as hell, but I swear she would definitely look better with me.

I leaned against the passenger side of my truck. "It's only a little after 10 now. Why are you getting ready for bed so damn early?"

Her arms were folded, and she rolled her big eyes. "Enough of that momma bullshit already. I didn't have to climb out of a window nor ask my damn momma to come downstairs, either. If you must know, I am having a major online sale tomorrow and I'm expecting to be up all night," she spat.

I grabbed her and wrapped my arms around her tightly, not giving a fuck that she had a man. I didn't even care if he was upstairs right now. In my mind, Keke would always be mine. "My bad, shorty! I didn't want anything. I just wanted you to know that I was wrong for snapping on you earlier. It's just that I didn't expect to still be feeling you after coming home from a bid."

She smiled. "I didn't expect you to either. I didn't expect to feel this way myself but look at us now."

"Yeah, yeah. If you're free after your sale, I would love to take you shopping. It's time to upgrade that wardrobe of yours. I've been some fire stuff you'll look good in."

"Mmmh. I have to see if I can squeeze you in," she teased but I wasn't going for that. "You know I'm not single these days!"

"Nah, shorty! It doesn't work like that and you know it. Text me when you are finishing working tomorrow and I'll be here to pick you up. Can you do that for me?"

She nodded her head. If I played my cards right, then I could have shorty breaking all the rules again, but this time it would be just for me. Fuck that drug game this time around!

***

CHAPTER SEVEN:
KEKE JONES
MOTHER AND DAUGHTER TALK

Work had been so hectic today due to half-price sale. In fact, there were several times I wanted to shut the whole damn site down because of how incompetent the customers were with me. The only way I made it through the sale is by thinking of Dollar.

Visuals of him leaning against his Mercedes truck last night would forever be etched in my brain. The way he hugged me last night, it made me feel protected from any unforeseen dangers. He had been texting me playful threats all throughout my sale, warning me to cancel whatever plans I had to spend the day with him. I proudly would be spending the day with him since Taylor was currently out of town on business anyways. In about two hours, I would've been around my crush.

My left eye immediately began twitching as soon as I pulled into my apartment complex. Now I wasn't the super superstitious type compared to my mom's side of the family, but there were two that I definitely believed to be true. One, if my right hand itched, then it meant that I would be coming into some money. Two, if my left eye twitched then it meant someone would make me mad. I cussed myself out for being so happy.

When I walked inside my place, my mom was sitting near the window. There was no telling how much she had learned about the complex from sitting right there due to the nice ass view I had.

"Hey ma, what's going on now?" I asked, kicking myself for letting her have a spare key. She was running the fuck out at this point.

She frowned up. "Don't speak to me! I should be asking why in the fuck you're out here slanging again. That bastard got you holding all of his work for a damn good reason! Yeah, the streets are fucking talking! He doesn't give a damn about you getting caught up. He's only protecting himself!"

The angel on my shoulder was telling me to respect her as my mom. While the devil on my shoulder was practically shouting, "put her in her damn place."

"Ain't no streets talking because they haven't seen me with Dollar, momma. The only damn street that's talking is these bum ass dudes in this complex. I know Demario told you because he was pressed the other day after he saw me with Dollar. Ain't nobody slanging no freaking drugs either! We're vibing like two grown ass adults and y'all can't stand it!"

And I finally understood why my left eye was twitching.

"You better be prepared to get hit with a federal charge that sticks this time!" she shouted.

Not in the mood to argue, I started to head back to my room so that I could find something to wear and shower for tonight. I was halfway out of the corridor when I heard my momma mumble, "Down ass bitch turned stupid ass bitch, if you want to.."

That was the straw that broke the camel's back. Ready to confront her, I spun around so damn fast.

"You know what? Ain't nobody being stupid. Well, not me. Y'all are mad at the same dude that protected and prevented me from getting a charge. And you know for yourself that Dollar has never wronged you. Sure, he doesn't have the ideal lifestyle but do we all? I'm sure you never thought you would see the day where his drug dealing money would also support you. It was all good until the feds raided him, right?"

Tears streamed down my face as I ran to my bedroom. I pulled my phone out of my purse and read the messages from Dollar. They were happy messages, but I was no longer in the mood to see him. These people really looked at Dollar like the bad guy and it was pissing me off. It made me realize how much I had been dodging him all because other people in my ear.

The message I composed read, "Something came up. Let's reschedule. I'm so sorry!"

I ended up not sending the message though. That would've given my mom all the satisfaction that she truly needed. She would've wanted me to cancel my plans. I wiped my tears, grabbed an outfit, and then hopped in the shower. It was time to put back on my bossed-up attitude with whoever!

***

"Damn, Keke! You look good as hell right now," Dollar complimented me.

"Thank you! This is actually Jazzy's old ass dress that she wanted me to wear." I gazed down at the dress that was very tight-fitting and was made on a tie-dye style. The dress was vivid so of course, it complemented my brown skin.

Dollar took me shopping in places that we used to go to all the damn time such as Saks Fifth Avenue. I swear I passed this store so many times after Dollar got locked up. Material things were no longer of value to me after all that shit went down.

"Find some shoes that you are comfortable walking in. I prefer heels over flats and tennis shoes," he whispered in my ear, where no one could hear. Dollar sat down on the bench, along with my shopping bags on the side of him. I went to the heels section and gazed at the various heels until I found a pair that I loved. They were heels by Steve Madden and the heel height seemed perfect.. As soon as I walked up to Dollar to show off my bomb ass heels, another woman walked up at the same time. She greeted me with a frown on her face. It didn't take long for me to figure out why she appeared to be upset. Shawty was pressed by my presence.

"Dollar, since when did you end things with me? And since when did y'all become a thing again," she spat, making direct eye contact with me. As much as I wanted to look away since I had become a much more chill person, I couldn't bring myself to do so.

"Misha, please don't start that shit. You know I'm not rocking with you like that." Dollar then faced me and asked. "Is that the only pair you wanted? If so, then I can pay and then we can get out of here."

I stood there trying to figure out what my next move would be. Dollar wasn't helping at all by trying to avoid her ass. Yeah, I noticed how he was ready to check out at this one store in particular. His ass was busted and didn't expect to be. In the other ones, he encouraged me to "shop til I drop." Dollar rose to his feet with all of my shopping bags in hand. The feminine shopping bags obviously caused the woman to frown up even more.

"Oh yeah, we taking disloyal bitches on shopping sprees now? Did I ever get a shopping spree for holding you down when she didn't? Does she know that you woke up in the middle of the night to come fuck me after your celebrating?"

"Oh, so you're the one he was texting that night?"

"Uhm, yeah!" she stated cockily.

You know the feeling you got when someone gave you bad news while you were eating? That's exactly how I felt right about now. Angry tears stung my eyes as I walked back to the shelf to put the heels back up. I no longer wanted the shoes nor anything else Dollar had purchased for me. I glanced to the side where Dollar and the chick were in the middle of a heated ass argument, which allowed me to slip out of the store undetected. I ran to the nearest restroom and called Jazzy to pick me up. As I waited for her, I went back into the shoe store hoping to find Dollar and that bitch. I realized that she called me disloyal when she was the scary bitch Dollar now had on his time. After I didn't see them in that store, I walked in and out of other ones, ready to run up on a bitch. At the same time, I was also saying that this shit wasn't worth it. I hope this wasn't a little payback for snapping on my mom in Dollar 's defense earlier. I believed in Karma and I knew how she worked, but I wasn't expecting her to come back that fast...

＊

CHAPTER EIGHT:
DOLLAR TATE
THUGS HAVE SOFT SPOTS TOO

Ideally, it wasn't a good look for a man to be sitting around in his damn feelings. It really wasn't a good idea to be in my feelings around my niggas inside of my traphouse.

"What's wrong with that pretty baby? Him heartbroken," Mon teased me.

We were all bagging up weed, breaking down cocaine and packaging pills. It was a busy night for us, which is why I took Keke shopping during the day because I knew I would be tied up with business later.

'Fuck you, Mon!" I shot back at him.

"Nah, but for real. What's wrong with you, Dollar? You're fucking up big time. You're miscalculating and shit. Come talk to me, big bro," Draco said. "You said we would be on top of our game once released. You off your square right now!"

Draco had been my like my right-hand man replacement once I went inside the pen. He made sure to stay in touch with my connect so that we would continue to supply the streets despite me not being in the streets. His loyalty ran so deep, people would've thought he had been there from the start.

He pulled me to the side and started questioning me.

"What's up with you, bro? It ain't like you to be fucking up when it comes to business. Is everything good with ya?" Draco questioned.

"These bitches don't know how to play their role, bro," I told him. "I took Keke out to the mall earlier and let her blow a couple racks. My treat! Everything was going fine until we went to the last store. Shorty picked out some heels and as soon as she came to show me them, guess who popped up?"

He shook his head as if he already knew the answer. "That damn Misha, I bet!"

"Bruh, yes! The bitch started running off at the mouth, saying she didn't know I replaced her ass. I tried my best to ignore her, but then she spilled the beans and told the whole damn store that we fucked after my celebration. The crazy part about it, Keke was standing right there the entire time."

"Damn, my nig. That's fucked up. These hoes be acting up."
"And we be letting them. What I should've done is choked her ass out in front of everybody." I felt myself getting angry all over again because she ruined a perfectly good day for me.

"Yeah, you should've. I'm surprised Keke didn't handle her ass."

"Man, I keep telling y'all that Keke is not the same Keke. She's a little bit calmer. Check this out though, she didn't see us, but I saw her ass looking for Misha. I had to force Misha to calm down by telling her that neither of us were prepared for Keke's ass beating."

Misha just didn't know that the reward would've been much greater if she would've acted like she didn't see me with another chick. I probably would've done something special like fucking her in the bedroom for a change. But nah, she just had to further ruin things between us. Most importantly, she may have ruined future plans for me and Keke.

"Have you tried contacting Keke after all that shit went down? Don't be silent because she will really think you're protecting Misha when it's really not that."

"That's the thing, I called her phone, but it would ring once and then go straight to voicemail. Do you think she blocked me?"

Draco nodded his head. "Yeah, she has blocked you for sure. You shouldn't have let her get away. I would've said fuck arguing with Misha and I would've chased after Keke. You know what they say..."

"Nah, I don't know what they say. What they say?" I asked out of curiosity.

"They say you only argue when you care which has a little bit of truth. So, if you were in the store going back and forth with Misha, then maybe you care about her after all."

I couldn't believe Draco had said some dumb shit like that.

"Alright, bet! So, let me guess, you care about Paris? Remember you just argued with shorty the other day about her trap-a-nigga pregnancy."

"Man, hell nah. You know I don't care about Paris's old ass. I just said that to fuck with you and it worked. On some real shit though, what are you going to do about Keke?"

"Man, I don't know. I tried calling her. She won't answer. I just know one thing,"

"What's that?" Draco asked.

"This shit better not push her deeper into the arms of her nigga. I'm telling you, Keke gon' be mine again. Period. It ain't nothing left in these streets for me. I'm sick of seeing the same hoes."

Draco smiled. "Exactly, my nigga! That's what I wanted to hear. That's why you should put your pride aside and go get her ass and make her listen to everything."

"As much as I really want to, we got so much business shit to handle. I don't have time to chase after Keke's dramatic ass right now. Plus, she may try to beat my ass since she didn't beat Misha's ass,"

"Chill, Dollar! I got everything under control like I did in the big house. If you want Keke just as bad as you say you do, which I know you do, then go pull up on her. I can handle all of this until the other boys get here," Draco said reassuringly.

"You sure?" I asked him, not wanting to put too much pressure on him.

"Go get your damn girl before I change my mind, bro," he joked, which he didn't have to tell me twice before I left my trap house and called Keke. As expected, she hadn't taken me off her block list just yet. I took a chance on driving to her apartment complex. I really needed to quit that shit just in case she came out with her dude. That sight would have been acting like male version of Misha.

As soon as I threw my car in park, Keke pulled up next to me as if she knew I was coming for her. I don't think she realized I was actually next to her though. I waited until she got out of the car before I got out behind her.

"Man, what the hell you are doing out so late?" I asked Keke, catching her completely off guard. I could slowly see her starting to relax her muscles. Mad or not, she knew she was protected in my presence.

"Oh, look at who it is, Dollar! The one that's spending money on me when he already has another bitch," she spat so venomously. She tried to walk off, but I lightly pulled her back. "You didn't tell me that was your woman!"

"You didn't ask plus shorty ain't my woman," was all I could think of.

She shook her head. "Well your groupie or my replacement or whatever you want to call her. That's why I blocked your number because I'm through with you. I should've known not to expect much from you after all this time had passed anyway," she fussed.

Seeing her get heated was actually a proud moment for me. She had all of her facts all wrong, though.

"Let me tell you something, I'm almost 28 years old. I'm very grown so I don't have to lie to you or anybody else. If I had a girl, then why would I spend my time trying to make you my girl? Huh? Shorty was just a federal fuck to me! I needed somebody to get me through those long ass days and nights. You did too but I'm not as mad as I should be--,"

"And you just expect me to believe that? Everyone in the store, I included, heard her say that you screwed her after your release bash. Why are you fucking with bitches that ain't your official bitch then, huh?"

Behind Keke's anger, I could see a bit of hurt. I was out here blocking my own damn blessing. I couldn't mess things up this time around! Nah, I couldn't. I licked my lips.

"Yeah, just like I thought, Dollar! You're only licking your lips to lubricate them lies you finna tell me," she shouted which caused me to erupt in laughter.

"Chill out, Keke. I'm not even fucking with her no more. She was something to do when there was nothing to do, but now I have you taking up my time. Just take a nigga off your block list and get these bags out of my car. Imma be embarrassed if I have to return all of these bags tomorrow and get my money back, especially in Saks Fifth. People gon' think I came home tryna stunt when I was really broke."
"Give it

to ol' girl. Oops, I forgot, she ain't earned shit. Not even my damn spot with her pathetic ass. She's lucky that I was so caught off guard and didn't drag her around that damn store."

"Hell yeah! I'm not gonna lie, I did tell her that. We saw you looking but I told her we better go into hiding if she couldn't hold her own. I still want you to have these bags regardless." I went back to my truck and grabbed all of her shopping bags with one hand. I spent close to 5 racks on her today, which was definitely nothing because I was a millionaire even after years of being incarcerated.

"Which apartment is yours again? Well, you can just lead the way and I'll follow for a change," I instructed.

Keke spun around so fast and tried to grab the bags herself. "No, no. It's okay. I'll take them inside myself. I can carry them, they're light bags."

I would've laughed if I didn't know what exactly she tried to avoid.

"That's interesting because not one time did you offer to carry any of your bags at the mall earlier. I'm not gon' put your momma in her place today or your boo, if that's the case," I smirked.

"I know that. It's just that I forgot to clean up my place the other night and I don't need you trying to judge me for it," she lied as she struggled to keep a straight face.

"Yeah, I like you better when you aren't lying. Baby girl, I'm not stupid. That was the dumbest excuse I've ever heard. Your mom is in there isn't she? Did she lose her place or something?" I questioned her.

"Yeah, my mom is in there. I'm not sure why she keeps popping up, but that's my momma. You only get one momma, right," she told me with an attitude. If only she could keep that same energy whenever her mom was on that bullshit with her.

"So, let me set your bags down while you pack an overnight bag for the night."

"An overnight bag for what? My house is right here and it's full of clothes."

Now, I was getting a bit annoyed with Keke's dumb ass questions. She answered everything with a question like a little ass kid. "You sure you met all of the requirements to graduate from your school, early at that?"

"Fuck you! Just follow me. Don't make too much noise because I don't feel like hearing some bullshit." Her voice was a tad bit shaky, which I really didn't understand why. I just hoped shorty didn't have a panic attack because it wasn't that damn serious to be running from her damn momma at her age. I was trying my hardest not to let this kill my vibe. Hell, I had more freedom in the pen than Keke did in the outside world, the free world.

We entered her small, studio apartment. Just about every light was on. I wanted to ask Keke how much her light bill was, but I decided not to. I didn't want to risk talking too loudly and disturbing her crazy ass momma. We successfully made it to her room without getting caught. I can't lie, a nigga felt like I was sneaking some chick into my house when I was back in middle school before I got hooked on Keke. We safely made it inside of her room, she locked the door then proceeded to pack an overnight bag without giving me too much sass.

"Can you grab my iPhone charger, please?" she asked while bent over tossing clothes in her bag. I had never got the opportunity to really see what Keke had behind her like I did just now. She definitely had grown up in all the right places. After grabbing her charger, I walked up behind her. My dick slightly brushed her ass. I was expecting Keke to be extra and fall over, but she didn't. She let out a few giggles.

"Boy, if you don't stop that," she threatened. "We are beyond that now."

"You like that, huh? I'm telling you, there is plenty more of where that came from."

And indeed, it was. I had been blessed in all aspects of my life; my anatomy included. My skin color resembled that of a Hershey Bar, which explained why I was so damn attracted to Keke because we both had that exotic look. I had a very muscular build and I was 6 feet even. You know, the basic things that made a woman go crazy. That was me, Dollar Tate.

"I'm done, let's get out of here," she demanded, ignoring everything else I had just said. She probably wasn't about that life anyway.

As soon as we got over the threshold, I let out a sigh of relief. We escaped without encountering her momma. I could get very disrespectful when disrespected so I'm glad that I didn't get a chance to see Keke's momma because it was obvious that she wasn't feeling me anymore.

***

We pulled up to my mini-mansion and I killed the engine.

"Wow, Dollar," she gasped while looking out the window in amazement. "You are really living the life. I don't think anyone returns to this after serving time. You are blessed, dude."

"Something like that. I hope you're feeling really special right about now because you're the first woman I've ever brought to my new home," I informed her.

That was the truth. Prior to getting locked up, I didn't let females come to my place of residence. I always came to theirs. Even though Misha had been something like my number one thing while locked up, she hadn't been to my new place either.

"Whaaaaaat? Not even your down ass bitch?" she asked in utter shock.

"She doesn't get special privileges and don't call her my down ass bitch. I'm not too sure if she is exactly that."

"Wow, I wonder if she knows that. With the way she was going mad hard, you would think that her position was secure," she said snidely followed by a chuckle.

Finally, we made it into the house where Keke was standing in the middle of the floor with her mouth wide open.

"Your house is goals and I haven't made it out of the foyer yet."

"Let me give you a tour then." I scooped her up in my arms and showed her my house. We finally stopped in my master bedroom where I gently placed her on my King-sized bed. I was definitely feeling some type of way. A way I didn't want to act on so soon considering the strain we sort of had.

"Do you miss messing with a man of my caliber?" I asked Keke out of piqued interest.

"Actually, I haven't messed with a man of your caliber since then, but I have always been reading about men with your old lifestyle," she blushed.

"Oh yeah, is that right? What happens when you read about the men like me?" I inquired, curious to know what went on inside of her mind. I wanted to know what she thought about my old lifestyle now without me directly asking her.

She sat Indian style on my bed, then placed her hands in her lap. "I don't even know why I'm about to say this. I don't need to be boosting your already big ass ego."

I took off my shirt, exposing the several tats I had. My top two were of a traphouse with a heart above it and an angel holding a ribbon with my grandma's name on it. I tossed the shirt on the floor. "You can say anything to me. I promise you; I've heard everything in the book. Nothing surprises me, shorty."

"I read to get my juices flowing. Not up there, but down there." She pointed at the center of her jeans.

"Oh yeah? You read those thug books by Wahida Clark or you read those freaky books by Zane?"

"I've never read a book by Zane. My dirtiest reads were by E.L. James -,"

"From The 50 Shades Trilogy," I laughed.

Her face broke out into a smile, exposing her Colgate smile. "O-M-G, how did you know they were by her?"

I shrugged. "I loved to read; it made the time go by much faster. Nobody knows this about me, not even my closest friends. You're the first person I've ever shared this with. I read all the books by her while incarcerated. That shit does get you going, huh?"

"So, I'm assuming you've seen the movies too?"

"Yeah. I did on the little tablets certain people get. That shit was worth every penny too."

"I'm ashamed to say this, but I pirated the movies. I mean, there are some movies you can't see in public because it makes you feel some type of way in private."

I wanted to hit her with a joke, but it was time to retire those jokes…for now.

"Hey, you gotta do what you gotta do. You ever re-enacted one of those sex scenes with your new nigga?"

She shook her head "no". "Not at all. I don't even know why I'm telling you this, but the sex is very vanilla."

"Get the fuck outta here, Keke. It's 2019. Ain't nobody just doing boring ass missionary nomo. Somebody's game is wack as hell. Y'all boring as fuck in the bedroom."

Completely offended, she said, "You talk a lot of shit for someone that was released almost two weeks ago. What's your dick game like now? I didn't have to wait on permission to have sex."
"I'm just fucking with you, Keke. Chill out and pipe the hell down sometimes!"

"As interesting as this topic is, I would like to go shower if you don't mind. Can you point me in the right direction?"

"My bathroom is right there, but if you don't feel comfortable taking a shower in the same room as me, you can go to the bathroom down the hall. I don't want you to get the wrong impression or anything like that."

I wanted to be extra cautious around her. I didn't want her to get the wrong perception of me since it had been years since we were last around each other. As much as I wanted to push up on her, I didn't want to come on too strong.

She grabbed her bag and said, "I don't mind showering in here."
Once I heard Keke hop in the shower, I went to the bathroom downstairs and showered myself.

"Fuck," I cursed when I looked down at the ever-growing boner, I had from Keke saying that her sex was vanilla. I knew shorty's pussy was good and hadn't been worked out in a good ass minute. As much as I wanted it, I knew I hadn't earned it again...yet. Had she been any of my regular hoes, she would've had to drop those panties. Switching the hot water too cold to get rid of my boner, I tried to clear all sexual thoughts of Keke. I brought her over to see if we could rekindle the friendship at least.

I returned to my room to find Keke sprawled out on my bed. It was only a little after 11. No matter how caged in I once was, I could never go to bed before midnight.

"I know yo' ass ain't getting ready for bed. It's just 11:10. You're such a damn granny," I teased her.

"Boy bye! Do you see this face? Do you see how flawless I am? That's because I mind my business, drink my water and most importantly, I know how to put my phone down and go to sleep at night," she clapped back.

That feisty-ness she was giving me right now, I brought that out of her.

"Okay cool. Suit yourself. I'm not going to bed anytime soon though."

I planned on getting my box of swishers out of my storage in my closet then heading to my man cave. I had gotten halfway out of the door when Keke called me.

"Dollar?" she called out; her voice was much softer now.

I turned around and looked at her. "What's up, Keke?"

"Uhm, how do you really feel about me being over here right now?"

That question definitely caught me off guard. I wasn't prepared to answer it because I knew how I truly felt about her being over here especially in that thin ass sleep set she had on.

"We really haven't kicked it much since we got here but I'm enjoying your company. I'm not gonna lie, I may be feeling it a bit too much, but I got some good ass self-control so you're good," I swear my response sounded something like a damn political response. How could I convince her of what I was saying when I didn't believe it my own damn self?

She real deal looked disappointment by my comment.

"Oh, okay," was all she said.

As much as I should've left the conversation at that, I was curious to know why she asked me something like that.

"Why did you ask? Are you bothered by being here or something?"

"I'm not bothered. It's just that I'm…ready."

"Ready for what, Keke?"

"I'm ready to take things to the next level with you. I've been ready since that night we ran into each other."

Now I had been getting my release on the regular before I got locked up.

Fuck! It's happening again. I thought to myself as I began to get hard all over again. Why was Keke trying me at this time of night?

I climbed next to her in bed. "Yo, where is all of this coming from? Talking about 50 Shades got you feeling some type of way, huh?"

She giggled and for the first time, I noticed that she had gained a tremendous amount of weight in her face which looked damn good on her.

"No, I've actually been thinking about this long before you brought up the movies. It's kind of embarrassing and so upfront. I just don't want to be labeled a hoe though."

"As much as I would love to, I can't go there with you right now shorty."

She frowned a bit. "Why not? Is it because you don't really think I'm feeling you like that?"

I chuckled at her question. "Nah, I think what we're both feeling is indeed real. If you were the average hoe, I would've bent you over by now. I just want to respect your relationship right now. I know if you were to give me that pussy right now, I would act a fool in it and be ready to put a title on shit. Our lives are too complicated right now."

She rolled her eyes, then got off the bed. "I just don't get it. You seem to like these hoes. Why is it that you can sleep with them, but you can't sleep with me? You don't give a fuck about their relationship status, so why do you give a fuck about mine? If you really cared about my status, then you shouldn't be involved anyways. You should be respecting the boundaries you're trying to set. Uhm, you can take me home now. I'm good on everything tonight."

I sucked my teeth because she was buggin' for no real reason right now. "You want to go home because I don't want to fuck? What type of shit is that? Use that big ass head that you have on your shoulders. C'mon now, you're smarter than this. I basically just said that I want to treat you like a lady and not like a hoe. Hoes don't get this special treatment that you're getting. Please go back to that Keke that didn't let a nigga fuck unless he had earned the right to do so. I like that Keke so much better."

Walking into my walk-in closet, I grabbed a t-shirt and a pair of sweats. I slipped the outfit on and put on my tennis shoes. I grabbed my keys and Keke's overnight bag at the same time.

"And just what do you think you're doing?" she had the nerve to ask with an attitude and her hands placed on her hips.

"I'm getting ready to take yo' ass home. I guess you're in the mood to wake yo' momma up and have her jumping all down my throat. I'm letting you know now that I'm not dealing with her bullshit tonight, so she better not come at me sideways."

"I'm not going anywhere, Dollar," she huffed.

"Are you sure about that? Cause I don't have time for this bullshit. Either you want to be grown or you want to be childish forever. Pick a side and stay there! I don't have no kids so I'm not dealing with no damn tantrum," I spat.

"Clearly, I am being grown. I just asked you to participate in something that grown folks do," she whined.

"Baby girl, you just don't get it. Not only will I fuck up your walking, but I'll fuck up your whole life. You're not ready for what all comes with me again. I'm telling you. And I'm not sharing no pussy, there is too much of it to go around. Nah, I'm good."

"I'll never know unless you tell me," she threatened me with a good time.

I sat next to her on the bed. "How do I explain this shit? I'm feeling you all over again, no lie. I'm readjusting to my new freedom, but I can't let that thug ass lifestyle go. I can't help that I'm a thug ass nigga. You feel me? The type of dude I am, they are no longer your type. I'm not used to messing with a chick that wants me to get up and work a normal 9 to 5. I'm 28, not 18. I want somebody with my mindset, a mindset of a hustler. I need my shorty to understand that I may be out making plays at 3:00, not someone who will go into panic mode when they realize I'm not in bed with them and start making emergency calls. No offense, but that type of person would be the new Keke and I can't get with that. It's too risky."

"So basically, you still want that ride or die type of chick after all this time?"

I shrugged. "That is more about skills than it is about a title, but essentially, yeah. If you're my official girl, then I need you to be down for the cause, I don't plan on leaving my old ways of making money behind. Not in this damn economy! If you ain't down for the cause, then I'll just treat you like a fuck buddy."

"That's all you had to say. You're talking to me as if I'm not used to the lifestyle, as if I've never been a part of that lifestyle with you. Damn, Dollar!"

"Bring yo' ass here," I instructed her. The Victoria's Secret sleep set she had on had started to get the best of me. I should've had more self-control when it came to her, but I couldn't. She was already irresistible from the moment I met her, but now she had become even more ravishing. I grabbed her small neck and slipped my long tongue into her mouth in an attempt to tongue kiss her. I was into it until she bit my tongue. I tried to keep kissing her until moved too damn fast again. Not wanting to risk having a painful, bleeding tongue, I broke the kiss.

I slapped her ass cheek. "Get that shit together. Don't give me no kiddie ass kiss. Where the spit at? Yo ass don' got slaw," I joked, causing her to laugh.

"Whew! It has been a hot ass minute," she responded shyly.

"First things first, as my woman you know you have to be confident. If you aren't confident in yourself right now, then how can I expect you to be confident in me...in us? Lesson #1, when I ask you something in regard to your sex life, I need you to be confident. You hear me?"

"Yes, Dollar."

"Nah, it is Dollar when we're outside this house, but it's daddy when we're behind these four walls. I got something else to kiss, though."

Pushing her onto the bed, I removed her silk shorts and spread her legs. She had a lil' bush down there that sort of discouraged me for a bit. But then I looked at it as if it was a Now & Later with some of the paper still left on it. Her pussy was about to get ate just like the Now & Later.

"Another lesson always keep this pussy waxed if you want me to touch it. If your last nigga liked a little hair, then that's him. By the way, end that shit as soon as possible,"

"Okay, daddy," she sang in a tune so sweet, not even Patti Labelle had shit on her.

I stuck my finger in her love hole. The way her walls tightly clamped down on my finger had confirmed what she had already told me. "You know when my tongue touches your clit, you lose all rights to it, right? That means no nigga can come during or after me. It's my duty to please your pussy while it's your duty to always clean it. Other than that, this right here belongs to daddy." Satisfied with her head nod, I went in for the kill. She gasped loudly in pleasure as my tongue went deep inside her as if I was a diver diving into deep waters. I maneuvered my tongue around inside her as her body violently shook underneath me. My tongue came inside with two goals: one, to find her g-spot and two, to make her cum. I curled my tongue as she loudly cried out in sheer pleasure, which was an indicator that I had successfully found her g-spot. I licked viciously as her body wiggled under me. Slowing down, I purposely let her get halfway up before I forcefully pushed her back onto the bed.

"Ne stop running and let me make love to this pussy," I whispered then started to lick her clit.

"Daddy," she moaned while massaging my head.

I looked up at Keke who looked like she was about to have a damn seizure. Her eyes were rolling into the back of her head. Never the one to brag and boast, but I definitely had Keke losing control as she climaxed. My goatee and nose were filled with her soaking wet juices which smelled like a mothafuckin' garden.

"You wanna taste yourself?" I asked her. I should've been selfish with Keke's pussy and not let her taste her own juices but then how would she know her juices tasted better than water?

She nodded her head.

"What the fuck did I just tell you?" I dropped to my knees but Keke quickly gained some sense. She yelled out, "Can I taste it, daddy?"

Satisfied with her answer, I leaned down and kissed her on her mouth. This time, she kissed me like she remembered who she was kissing many years ago.

"Mmm, mmm fuckin' good, right?" I imitated the old Campbell's Chicken Noodle Soup commercial.

We both burst into laughter. As much as I wanted to sample Keke's love tunnel right now, I decided not to. After passionately making love to her pussy, I was ready to assault it. With it being her first time in a long time, I couldn't do her like that. I didn't want to rearrange her organs on the first time in a long ass time. So, I slipped her shorts back on like a gentleman would and we climbed in bed together. She snuggled up next to me, making sure her ass was on my dick. Shortly after, she drifted off to sleep, leaving me up with yet another damn boner. Fuck!

***

3:00 A.M.

I woke up out of my sleep when I felt a body pressed up against mine. I had forgotten that Keke had stayed the night with me that fast. I was used to sleeping alone after having to do it so damn long, so this was all new to me. This time of the morning is when I would usually get horny. As convenient as it was to roll over and wake up Keke, I couldn't do it. I wanted to wait for her. That was my word and I was definitely sticking it to.

So, I sent Misha a text on some "what you are doing, can I come through" type of shit. Yeah, I know I said I was done fucking with Misha and that was true. But I didn't say I was done fucking with her pussy, not right now at least. She had almost two months left before I cut her off, that's when Keke would have to let me know if she was on some getting serious shit. Though the pussy was good as fuck, I couldn't give her my dick without knowing that she was actually mine. Well, assuming that I could really wait that long, I wouldn't give her no dick in the meantime.

I kid you not, it hadn't been a good minute since I sent the text and Misha was telling me bring my dick by. "Do hoes ever really sleep?" I asked myself. Maybe she kept her phone on loud or something. I wasn't complaining though because I had a nut dying to be released.

I slipped out of bed, careful not to wake Keke up. Hurriedly, I went into my bathroom to wash my face and brush my teeth again. I swear I did both in under one minute because I didn't want to give my conscience time to fuck with me and talk me into staying in bed. One thing was for sure, I would be back home long before the sun came up and long before Keke woke up.

After stopping at the store to buy a pack of Magnums, I had finally made it to Misha's duplex.

"Wassup, Dollar?" an unfamiliar dude greeted me. He was outside with a few other niggas. I wasn't intimidated at all because none of them looked like a threat. If anything, they were bums for being outside at this time of morning, passing a blunt back and forth. Personally, I wouldn't be out if I wasn't sliding up in some pussy or getting money. Maybe that's why I was put in the position I was in right now. Not too many niggas had my mindset, obviously. I nodded my head and then continued up the short steps to Misha's place.

This time, she opened the door wearing a robe that was way too short. It was much better than her being butt ass naked, that's for sure. Walking into the living room, I observed the layout of it. There were mini-lit candles on the coffee table with red rose petals sprinkled along the floor as well. Inwardly, I chuckled at her efforts to turn the living room into a bedroom plus bathroom. The gesture was cute but very unwanted. I was here to fuck her not make love to her.

Dropping her robe, Misha strutted over to me. She went for my shorts and boxers until she released the monster inside of them. We both made eye contact as she used her tongue to moisturize my head. As soon as she shoved my dick in her wet mouth, my mind drifted back to Keke who I had left at home. A few hours ago, I was claiming ownership of her pussy. Now, I was out here giving away dick that should've been hers, despite me not telling her that it indeed was hers. I wondered had she noticed that my side of the bed was now empty. Our relationship had barely gotten started before I started being disloyal behind her back.

I grabbed a fistful of Misha's crunchy weave and pulled her head back to get her off my dick. "Stop shorty, I can't even do this right now."

Almost instantly, there was a flash of hurt in her eyes. "You can't do what?"

I sighed. "I can't do this...I can't let you give me head and I damn sure can't fuck you."

"I know it isn't because of that disloyal ass girl I caught you with in the mall," she responded, visibly upset now.

Proudly I admitted, "Yep! That's exactly why. I can't cheat on her."

She went back for my stick. "If that's the case, then you cheated on her when you said you were on your way over. Besides, you can't name a damn thing she has done for you ever since you were released! NAME ONE!"

Now that had totally caught me off guard. I wasn't expecting Misha to have a comeback for that. She said it so fast, it was as if she had rehearsed that line plenty of times. Unfortunately, she was right. If I had no intention of fucking Misha, then I shouldn't have text her or brought my ass over here. So, I let her resume by giving me some of that sloppy, A1 head.

Like I said, I wanted to wait until Keke was serious about becoming official. Until then, my dick had to stay occupied...

* * *

CHAPTER NINE:
DEMARIO SANDERS
STREET ENVY

"I just can't get over how Dollar couldn't open his damn mouth and speak to you last night. If it's one thing I can't stand, it's an uppity ass nigga especially one like him after his ass has been gone for years. That shit is for bitches," My homie, Tony, said.

He was right. Last night, I spotted Dollar 's G-Wagon pull up outside of the duplex I sometimes hung out at. I already knew it was him because nobody else in the city of New Orleans drove a metallic Porsche that changed colors. I don't know what made me speak to that fool, but I did. He nodded his head and went to Misha's door. Misha was a ran through thot, but she had slowed down tremendously since fucking with Dollar. How did I know that? Because she used to give me and my niggas the pussy at the same time. Now running a train on her had become impossible. She didn't want to give up none of that "choo-choo" anymore.

"Aye, didn't you say that he was back fucking with your neighbor too?" Tony asked me.

"I forgot about that shit! Hell yeah, they got something going on again. I had already claimed shorty from the start when she moved over there but she claimed that my lifestyle was too dangerous."

I found it backward how Keke didn't want to give me any play, but she was back hanging out with a notorious drug dealer. On the other hand, I was just getting started, but I planned to takeover.

"As much as I despise Dollar, I gotta give it to him, he's that nigga. That man managed to ruin his operation straight out of prison. On top of that, the nigga came home and was still relevant. That's some true King type shit!"

I sucked my teeth in disgust. "He won't have all of that for long," I said reassuringly.

"Yeah, as a man, he can't have everything the world has to offer."

"Exactly, my nig. I want his trap house, his car, his bank account and most importantly, Keke. She's so innocent. I would love to turn her ass out."

Tony chuckled. "Basically, you want Dollar's life."

"Hell yeah, I do," I proudly admitted. "I want his life and I want his head, too. His ass has been disrespectful since day 1. I still haven't gotten into his birthday bash prior to the release one, he didn't speak to me and now he's probably back fucking the last good girl on Earth."

"You're still holding on to a grudge from ten years ago, I see."

Indeed, I was still holding on to that grudge. Growing up, school wasn't for me. By eighth grade, I had dropped out. The day I turned 15, my mom took the day off from work. Instead of celebrating my birthday, I got a work permit. She took me around the city and made me apply to all of the fast food restaurants. Eventually, I landed a job at McDonald's as a cook. I flipped burgers and then came my desire to flip some real money. I knew the real money was where my mom tried to keep me out of and those were the streets. I was able to slang a lil' dope here and there, but it wasn't enough to make me quit my job at McDonald's, however.

I continued to grind. Years had passed and I was still stuck slanging here and there. When I turned 18, rumors of the youngest cat had begun to run New Orleans and shit. He was Dollar. At the age of 20, he had already flown out of the country to meet the connect. Many street niggas envied him, especially the older ones who were in the same boat as me. However, I secretly admired Dollar. He was the youngest in charge and I eventually wanted to be, too.

The thing is, he wasn't allowing new niggas into his camp. I had never asked him personally, but I kept my ears to the streets. Everybody wanted to be down with Dollar, but Dollar made sure he didn't let anybody in his circle.

The night of his first birthday bash was a night I would never forget. He had turned 20. The nigga had the entire parking lot on swole. Bitches were getting in for free. While niggas had to pay $50 for entry, on top of that, he had security out there checking niggas for weapons, which I didn't have to worry about. I had my last $50 ready to spend just to be in the same building as that nigga. I guess the security sensed my excitement because I got called a "paper gangsta" and turned around at the door. Since then, I've never tried to attend his bash again. So yeah, I was holding a grudge.

"I keep telling you, I'm ready to handle that nigga whenever you are."

"We gotta stick to the plan, Tony! Our first step is to hit him in his pockets. The only way we can do that is by fucking with his traps."

"Yeah, that nigga got so many traps scattered throughout New Orleans now. How will we know when to strike?"

"His people can't patrol every trap at the same time. I been watching how they move for months now. He has way more security at the main trap. The smaller ones, he doesn't really give too many fucks about. I don't see too many cats coming in and out of those," I informed him.

"Well shit, I'm down either way. We just gotta make sure we recruit enough niggas just in case."

"Fasho! You know mothafuckas on my side of town are always money hungry and are always looking to make a quick buck. I can round up about 5 guys. Match me!"

"I gotcha, bro. I can get on that now. I got two twin cousins who have been shooting since they were youngins."

"We definitely need them on our team then."

It wouldn't be long before I was on top. All I had to do is wait for the perfect time to strike. Dollar had reigned supreme for ten years now. It was time for somebody to step up and stop him. I was the underdog, but I had so much to prove.

***

CHAPTER TEN:
JAZZY JACOBS
FEELING JAZZY

"Right there. Don't stop, Draco," I moaned.

Draco had my legs pinned behind my head. I always knew I was flexible because I was a majorette back in High School. On top of that, with previous dudes I've been with, I could hit a split on the dick. However, I've never had my legs pinned like this before. There was a mixture of pain and pleasure as Draco fucked the shit out of me.

"Look at you. I thought you could keep up. I got your legs shaking and shit," he groaned in my ear as he continued to fuck me senseless.

Finally, he released the tight hold he had on my legs. I thought he was going to give me a few seconds to recoup at least, but he flipped me over and demanded that I get on all fours. I arched my back perfectly to give him better access to the kitty. He slid his way inside of me and paused for a minute. Stealing a glance at him, I saw him biting down on his lip. That was all the confirmation I needed to know that my pussy was still good. I used this as an opportunity to throw it back on his dick. I wanted to show out, but Draco wouldn't let me be great.

He slapped my ass then bit it. "Chill out. I'm in control, Jazzy." He pulled out of me and entered me quickly, without warning, making me lose my perfect arch.

"Owww!" I cried out in pain. Draco was packing. His dick was long and thick like those Hillshire Farm sausages. I'm telling you, a dildo or a strap-on could compare to this real thing.

"Don't cry now. Shut the hell up and take this dick," he fussed as he started moving fast in and out of me.

Unable able to take it anymore I cried out, "I'm cumming, Draco."

"Cum on this dick then," he shouted while I felt my juices coat his dick.

A few seconds later, he came right behind me. I could feel every seed he released inside of me.

That is when reality set in. Panicked, I stuck my hand inside of my love tunnel and tried to get his nut out of me. I heard Draco chuckling.

"It's too late, shorty. Ya pussy really swallowed all of it."

"Draco, this shit isn't funny. You did wear a condom, right?"

He slipped back into his jeans. "Yeah, I really did put on one. What's wrong? You're clean, right? I'm for sure clean. I stay at the clinic now that I'm a free man again. You saw my last panels, don't play!"

"Hell yeah, I'm clean. Just because I'm freaky doesn't mean I'm reckless. No STDs or viruses over here," I boasted. I had never fucked a nigga without a condom before. Draco was the first to hit it without rubber which is crazy considering how skeptical I was of him at first.

"Okay then, so why are you freaking out? You're good." He leaned down and planted a kiss on my forehead. I only panicked because I knew for sure that I wasn't on any birth control. I quit getting my depo shots after I got in a relationship with Tanya. There was no need to be on birth control if I wasn't getting the D like that. Besides, the first shot had given me so many complications. I swore after my last injection that I wouldn't get back on birth control and I didn't. If Draco wasn't afraid of getting me pregnant, then I shouldn't have been afraid myself.

"So, what do you have planned for the rest of the day?" I questioned him.

He fake pouted, making him look more handsome than ever. "Damn shorty, you're ready to get rid of me already? I wanted to kick it with you."

"I'm glad you want to chill with me. I didn't want you to leave in the first place, but I do think I need to go soak in the tub."

"I guess I should say thank you. It was a privilege to beat that thang up. Do you need me to run to the store and get some Epsom salt? I can if you want me to."

"Yes, please. I would gladly appreciate it."

"Bet, shorty." As soon as Draco walked out of my apartment, I got up while still butt ass naked and started twerking. Walgreens wasn't far from where I lived so I decided to call up my best friend. She answered on the first ring.

"Damn bitch. What, or should I say who has you so occupied that you haven't been in contact with your best friend?"

"Girl, I been trying to be an adult for a change and not always run my mouth. Dollar came over to my place last night and made me stay the night with him."

"Ooh, bitch," I cheered. "What happened between y'all last night? Did you get that prison dick this time?"

I felt like a proud mama hearing that Keke finally stayed with Dollar. She had been looking for ways but was scared of Taylor popping up unexpectedly and wanting to surprise her since he was away for months with work. I felt even better knowing that it was with Dollar that gave my bitch her groove back and not some dude who loved to spend his leisure time picking up books in the library. I was watching Keke re-blossom right before my eyes and I knew Dollar was to blame like always!

I could hear Keke laughing. "No, bitch! I didn't get the prison dick you keep asking about, but he went down on me. The nigga still knows how to put in work. Whew!"

"Sis, I can't believe I'm talking to you right now. Wasn't it around this time last year that you said you were finally over him? So, what's gon happen with these rekindled feelings and shit?"

"Honestly, Jazzy, there is something about Dollar that makes me want to stand by him no matter if the general public ain't feeling us like they used to. There's just something about him.

"Oh yes honey, you're back using his lingo too. Yo' ass is starting to sound just like him and Draco. You should thank me, though."

"Uh, thank you for what exactly?" she had the nerve to ask.

"For dragging your ass out to the club with me that night. Otherwise, I highly doubt you would've rekindled things with Dollar. Yo' ass would've still been stuck in the house reading about those men like Dollar. Now you have a real one, instead of a damn book bae," I laughed. "It's about time you ditched Taylor ass too."

"Screw you! You may have drug me to the club but I'm the one who initiated all contact again but thank you. So how are you and Draco?"

"You asked a perfect time. He just finished bussing down my walls not too long ago. Now he's at Walgreens getting me some Epsom salt to soak in."

"I know it's been a minute since you've felt some penis, but please, whatever you do, don't end up pregnant. Remember, we want to take over the world eventually."

Before I could respond, I heard her Dollar yelling in the background. "Keke, get your ass fine here."

"That's bae! Look, I gotta go. I'll call you back --,"

I rolled my eyes at Dollar 's demanding ass. "Bitch, you better not get off this phone. You haven't had that dick in years and you neglecting me already."

"I said I'll call you back, Jazzy." She quickly hung up, leaving me wondering what the hell was going on over at her place. Sooner or later, her ass would be bagging up dope while taking that same dope dick like she did in the past.

***

CHAPTER ELEVEN:
KEKE JONES
MY MOMMA DOES NOT UNDERSTAND

After my mom tried to bash me, my day had continued to plummet. I swear that woman could put me in a bad mood. Don't get me wrong, I loved my mom, but I definitely disliked her parenting style. I disliked her controlling ways. It seemed like the older I got, the more she tried to tighten this invisible leash around my neck. I didn't know if I would ever be able to break loose or suffocate at the hands of her. The only time I enjoyed myself is when I was around Dollar. It was sad that I couldn't enjoy myself in my own home or even around Taylor now who was my boyfriend. Hell, if anything, I felt like a damn prisoner in my own home.

Right now, I was in the middle of applying for a business loan in order to obtain a store. I wanted a physical business instead of just an online business too. That way, I could increase my income. Luckily, I started building my credit score after Dollar got locked away since I would no longer have his cash to buy anything. My credit score wasn't perfect, but it was better than what it had been. I had put in my application and was now waiting on an approval. I went to sit down and then I heard,

"Don't I know you?" the woman asked with a slight attitude. Mind you, she still had her oversized sunglasses on so I couldn't tell who was behind the sunglasses. I didn't remember faces, especially if you weren't relevant. Unfortunately, a lot of people were irrelevant to me.

I tried to give her the benefit of the doubt by saying, "Ma'am, I don't know you or any other of these faces in here. I came here to handle my business and leave."

She laughed while ripping off her sunglasses. "Now do you remember me, bitch?"

Oh, now I did. It was the lil' cocky bitch from the mall. How could I ever forget her name? How could I forget that she looked like a damn amazon, too? My heart was thumping fast. I can't lie, she had me shook at her mighty boldness. If I could avoid conflict, then I was going to do just that. This was such a professional setting and I really needed that money, so I needed to play my part.

"Ma'am, this is not the time or place. Okay? At least let's wait until we're outside of here. Then we can handle whatever issues you may have like an adult would."

"Dollar could never be with your disloyal ass again! That man belongs to me, bitch. I'm the one that held him the fuck down, you didn't!"

WHAP!
WHAP!

She delivered a few slaps to my face. I wasn't a weak bitch by any means and I really wanted this loan, but this bitch had me fucked up. I politely asked her to wait, but she wouldn't. I let her disrespect me the first time out in public, but it wouldn't be a next time. I drew back and began raining blows on her. I was about to kick her dead in her smart-ass mouth until I felt my body being held in the air. I knew it was one of the employees of the lending companies.

I heard the employee say, "Ma'am, you both have 5 seconds to leave this premise before the cops arrive. Attacking people isn't allowed here."

"I'll leave. Tell that bitch to stop messing with my man," she barked before I heard her storm out and her tires screeching off.

I was carried back inside the building where I was given a towel to clean my face. The employee's face was beet red, and I immediately became ashamed.

"Do you mind telling what happened back there?"

I shrugged. "Honestly, I don't know what happened back there myself. I tried to give her the benefit of the doubt and then she started attacking me." I purposely left out the part about us being involved with the same man.

"Yeah, but she said some expletives back there and said stop messing with her man. You're wanting this loan to start a business, right? This kind of behavior isn't consistent with someone wanting to own a business."

I nodded my head "yes". "Of course, I know that. I didn't start with her, she started with me."

"And you couldn't avoid confrontation by simply walking away?" he had the nerve to ask. I swore his kind of people always thought matters could be resolved by simply walking away. It was much easier said than done.

"Mr. McKinney, I tried to walk away. How could I when she immediately began attacking me? I had every right to defend myself." My voice cracked. I didn't want to cry, but this was all fucked up.

"Due to your actions, I have no other choice but to use discretion when it comes to approving you for the loan. At this time, we can't offer funding for your rising business."

"So, because of her actions, I can't get a business loan," I asked. He nodded his head.

"But she started it. Why would I start drama in a setting like this? I've never done anything like this before, but she forced my hand."

"I know that, Ms. Jones. But you have to understand if this gets back to the district manager, or worse, corporate, then I could be fired off the rip. As much as I want to be generous, I have to follow our company's guidelines when it comes to those we want to lend to. I'm sorry!"

Tears blurred my vision, as I ripped my loan application and gathered my things. I had just lost a source of future income because Dollar couldn't keep his hoes in check. No longer sad, but now furious, I contemplated calling Dollar 's phone on some dumb, reckless shit. Better yet, I decided to pull up on him.

***

Without so much of a notice, I pulled up to his house. I rang the doorbell and waited for him to come to the door. It seemed like the longer I waited for him to come to the door, the more I became upset. What seemed like an hour later, the door finally swung open. Dollar was standing before me in a robe.

"What's up, Keke-"

WHAP!

I slapped him dead in his mouth before he could finish saying my name. "Don't 'what's up' me. I just got denied for a major business loan because your bitch came to me on some stupid ass shit. She attacked me because of your ass." I tried to slap him some more, but he pinned my wrists against the wall.

"Yo, what the fuck are you talking about? Who told you that you could lay your mothafuckin' hands on me, girl?"

I looked down at the robe that was now open due to us tussling. My eyes landed right on Dollar 's dick. He was erect while I was in total shock. The size was so damn abnormal.

"You like what you see, huh?" he whispered in my ear. Squirming, I tried to escape from his grasp, but he wouldn't let me. Instead, he pressed his body further into mine. His dick was a little bit above my waist. I could feel the same wet sensation forming in my panties.

Dollar took the robe off and let it drop to the floor. He scooped me into his arms and took me to the first bedroom on the hall.
He went for my pants.

"No, Dollar! This is over. I just got attacked because of your dumb ass games," I fussed. Dollar placed his hand over my mouth as he pulled my pants and panties off. It was a good thing I had put my Nair to use this morning. He looked down at my pussy and started smiling.

"Nah shorty, we ain't gon' ever end," he sang as he pushed a finger inside of my wetness. As much as I wanted to keep resisting, the feeling of his finger made me stop.

In between kisses, he said, "No worries, baby. I'll take care of Misha as soon as I finish taking care of this pussy."

He spread my legs and lowered himself at my waist. He opened my labia and rubbed his fingers down there, then brought his hand up to my face.

"You see that?" He referred to the clear substance on his fingers. "Your pussy dripping for me, ma."

I was enjoying it until I felt his dick resting on top of me. Immediately, my body tensed up.

"You gotta relax, Keke. Otherwise, it is gonna hurt since it's been a hot ass minute. Well, it's gonna hurt anyway because of my size but by relaxing, it will cut the pain down in half. Attempting to relax, I awaited his next move. Initially, I expected him to go inside but he surprised me when he got down on his knees and started licking like a thirsty dog. Before I could even get really into it, he stopped licking. I could feel his head at my opening.

"Dollar, please use a condom," I begged, afraid of any consequences that were associated with unprotected sex. I didn't want any STDs, nor did I want to get pregnant.

"This dick is clean, ma! I have not hit a chick without a rubber since I've tested since being released. You're about to be the first."

"But what about me getting pregnant? You forgot about that."

"And? What about it? You're grown. It's normal for women to have kids at your age. You're just trying to avoid getting this dick. I don't fall for distractions, I'm too woke for that," he chuckled.

There was no winning with Dollar, so I shut my mouth and closed my eyes.

A few minutes of pleasure is not worth years of pain. My mom's voice echoed in my head. I wanted to stop Dollar and strap up, but it was too late.

"Ouch!" I cried out in pain when I felt the tip of his dick enter me.

"Relax, Keke. I still have a lot more to put in. Take your mind off the pain," he instructed. While he slowly, yet painfully entered me, he began to suck on my nipples. Eventually, I started to relax as he slowly moved in and out me. With every stroke, I felt my poor walls being stretched.

My "ows" soon turned into "oohs". There were tears of pain and pleasure sliding down my face.

"Fuck, this pussy is so tight, ma!" he moaned in my ear. It was the first time I had ever heard him moan. The sound of a man moaning definitely turned me on even more. "I know I won't be able to last much longer."

…And he didn't. By the time I came, Dollar surely followed.

Dollar scooped me in his arms and took me to the shower. I couldn't believe I had given him the pussy again after almost 5 years and got attacked by that crazy ass girl which she definitely lost that battle. The good had outweighed the bad, in this case.

"Do you want me to run to the store and get a pad just in case you bleed some more? I don't think you will since it's light, but a nigga went beast mode and it had been a minute," He asked, interrupting my thoughts.

"Thanks, but I have one in my purse."

"You still don't use tampons, right?"

"Hell no! I didn't want anything up me that will be able to give me septic shock ..."

He smirked. "Yeah, until now! On a serious note, don't sweat that petty ass loan. You're too young to be putting yourself in debt like that. I got you, regardless. When I said that years ago, I meant that shit no matter what!"

Jazzy would've loved to be in my position right now. She always said that she wanted a man to take care of her, so she didn't have to work.

"As nice as this gesture is, I can't. Don't you know that all hell would break loose if my mom found out you funded my actual brick-and-mortar store? She knows I don't have the funds to do something like this."

"Excuse me, but I don't give a fuck about that lady's opinion and you shouldn't either. She keeps saying that you because you keep letting her. Hell, you can take my offer and move in with me. Let her live in your apartment since she can't seem to stay away from it too long. I'll foot the bills my own damn self just to get her to shut up. I'll do anything for you to be the same nonchalant Keke that loved a nigga before I got locked away and these people fed you these dumb lies about me. You can't give me the pussy like you're feeling me but you're letting these people diss me. It's time to stop letting people convince you that I somehow wronged you. It's now or never or I can't rock with you. Simple!"

I thought Dollar was joking, but the serious look on his face had told it all. He was dead ass serious. I didn't want to lose Dollar to some bullshit. He had always been the best part of my life. I mean, we got our passports together, matching whips together, and all that stuff. We experienced things together for the first time together.

"Okay cool," was all I could say. Even I didn't know exactly what I meant by that.

"It's okay to be making your own decisions and not apologizing for it. That's why you get older, not younger." He planted a kiss on forehead. Dollar walked out the bedroom, leaving me alone with my thoughts.

***

CHAPTER TWELVE:
DOLLAR TATE
HOES GOING TO BE HOES

Now I knew hoes didn't have respect for others simply because they didn't have any respect for themselves. Even still, that didn't give Misha the right to attack Keke. Misha was in no position to be laying hands on any of the chicks I fucked with, simply because she wasn't mine and I damn sure wasn't hers.

The last thing I wanted is for Keke to have to be knocking with hoes over me. She didn't deserve that, and I wasn't going to put her through that. We didn't even go through that shit back in the day because bitches automatically knew what was up! Starting today, all of my hoes had been fired. Once I got a feel of Keke's pussy again, then it was pretty much over for Misha, Naudia, and everybody else involved.

We pulled up to Misha's duplex. Sure enough, she was at home.

"I know you don' changed and all. You aren't extra sensitive, are you?" I asked Keke.

"Only when it comes to people I care about. I don't give a fuck about nobody else, especially that bitch in there." She nodded her head towards Misha's spot.

"That's what I'm talking about, give me some."

She parted her lips and allowed me to tongue kiss her. Yeah, I had turned into a sap for her ass all over again just that fucking fast.

"Let me do all of the talking, okay? You don't have anything to worry about. This is all in my hands now. You handled it earlier, now let me handle it," I commanded.

We got out the car and I led the way up the short steps. I knocked on the door. As soon as Misha opened the door, I punched her square in the mouth. Nah, I didn't give the trifling bitch a chance to plead her case because she didn't give Keke enough time to walk away.

CRACK!

I heard the sound of her teeth being knocked out. Grabbing her by the hair, I drug her through the same living room I had started to fuck her in.

"Close the door, Keke," I instructed. "Who the fuck gave you permission to attack Keke. Huh, bitch? You lost your damn mind and I came to help you find that mothafucka."

"I'm sorry, Dollar. I didn't mean to," she cried as blood spewed onto the floor along with her missing front tooth. Her breath smelled like shit due to the bleeding.

Tightening the grip on her weave I said, "You didn't mean to what? You didn't mean to get yo' ass handed to you for fucking with what's mine? You expected me to be okay with this? It's Keke before all you hoes. I told you from the start, all you had to do is play your part."

"Please," she begged.

I snatched the gun out of my waistband and forced it into her mouth.

"Please what, kill yo' ass for that foul ass stunt? You got her denied because you couldn't handle being just a piece of pussy. Fuck that!"

"Dollar, no!" I heard Keke yelling behind me.

"Shut the fuck up, Keke! I told you to let me handle it the way that I want to. I know you don't feel sorry for this worn-out, tired ass bitch! She didn't feel sorry for you when she attacked you out of nowhere and got your ass denied. So, don't feel sorry for her," I spat.

"I said that's enough, Dollar! Let's fucking go," she yelled. "Let the tired bitch live."

I turned around to face Keke. "Yo, are you fucking serious right now?"

"I'm dead ass. So, let's go!"

I should've shoved the barrel of my gun down Misha's throat because I felt her punishment was too light. The only thing that saved her is Keke and the fact that a murder charge would look good on me right now.

I removed the gun from her mouth. She started coughing dramatically for no damn reason. "Bitch, you got lucky! You better thank Keke for saving your life because today was sure about to be your last day. I'm not fucking playing. Thank her right now. If the shit isn't heartfelt then I'm offing your ass right here, right now. Keke won't be able to save you either."

"Thank you so much for saving my life, Keke. I am so sorry about what happened earlier. I will not bother you anymore. I'm sorry and I knew better than to get involved with Dollar."

"Good, bitch! Cause the next time, I won't be so nice about it. And another thing, Dollar belongs to me if you didn't get the memo already. That's been my dick for years, lil' bitch!"

There was so much fire in Keke's eyes that I had never seen before. It made me wonder if she really wanted to spare Misha's life like she claimed.

"And you already know to keep your fucking mouth closed, right?" Misha nodded her head. Her face was covered with blood, tears, and snot. She sure didn't look like the same bitch who used to be happy to freely give that pussy to me.

I slapped Keke on the ass. "Let's go, baby!"

"Since when did you learn to claim a dick like that, baby?" I asked Keke when we returned to the car.

"I don't know. It just came out of nowhere. Although it was the truth, it just rolled off my damn tongue," she laughed.

"Keep that tough shit up, because you know just how I like that shit! That shit is such a turn on, for real."

"Not as much as you are riding hard for me. Now that was a complete turn on."

"Keke and Dollar, huh? I like the sound of that. Those names sound good together all over again."

She unfastened her seat belt and climbed to the driver side.

"Oh, is that right? But does this feel good though?"

Shorty pulled down her yoga pants and then pulled my dick out my basketball shorts. After struggling for a minute, she finally sat on it. She was about to fuck a nigga in broad daylight. In that moment I knew, I had my old Keke back! That woman right there? That was my down ass bitch!

***

CHAPTER THIRTEEN:
JAZZY JACOBS

After days and days of messing around, Draco finally dropped me off at my place because he said that he had some business to take care of. Honestly, I didn't mind because I had become extremely sore and super dry from us constantly fucking. I needed to give my coochie time to rehabilitate itself or I was another fuck away from running to the emergency room. I had definitely met my match in the bedroom that's for sure.

I was now doing laundry since I literally had no clean panties left due to messing with Draco. Either they had become soaked due to being aroused by Draco or me constantly fantasizing about Draco when he wasn't around me. I put my first load in the washer at the same time there was a knock on my door. I knew it wasn't Keke because she had been on Dollar 's dick hella hard lately and I knew she wasn't getting off anytime soon.

Damn, Draco misses me already. I thought to myself.

I opened the door with a smile but that smile quickly faded when I spotted the last person I wanted to see, Tanya.

"Uhm, Tanya what are you doing here?" I definitely could've gone to my grave without ever seeing her again. On some Flavor Flav shit, her time with me was up for real.

Standing before me looking like Cleo from "Set it Off", she had the nerve to lick her lips.

"Damn, baby. You don't miss me?"

"Obviously not. It's been a few weeks since you stormed out of my place. I didn't hit you up, did I? I thought maybe you would've gotten the memo. After all, you basically told me that you had a lot of hoes. So why are you here now?"

"You know I was letting you cool off. I only came here to bring you that thing that you like."

"Okay, and what is that? I sure don't see anything in your hands. Maybe you got the cash in your pockets then." Other than Draco's dick, money was something that I most definitely liked.

She chuckled. "Don't I always make sure your bills are paid, regardless? That's not what I'm talking about."

"Then what are you talking about?" I asked, growing impatient with her childish ass games.

She flicked her tongue. "I bet now you know what I'm talking about."

I shuddered at the thought of getting head from Tanya after getting head from Draco. Draco was so gentle and meticulous when it came to eat my pussy. He treated it like a delicate flower. Whereas, Tanya was aggressive as hell. She ate the pussy roughly like a predator eating its prey. At first, I was content with it because she could still make me cum…sooner or later. Now that I had been introduced to proper pussy eating, of course, I didn't want to go back to getting my pussy crunched and munched on.

"Nah, I'm good Tanya. I think I'll pass on that."

I tried to close the door on her, but she quickly pushed it back open. She came in and pinned me against the door.

"Say, what the hell is wrong with you? You haven't seen me in weeks and you're still acting funny. Now you don't want to give me none of my pussy."

I rolled my eyes at her. "Girl, boy, this is not your pussy. The last time I checked, it was attached to my body and not yours."

"You know what the fuck I mean when I say this is my pussy. I pay the water bill so that you can clean this pussy, right? I pay the electric bill so that you can see this pussy, right? You're my bitch, therefore this is my shit."

Using one hand, she stuck her hand in my boy shorts. She had my wrists pinned with the other hand. She felt around in my shorts and clearly, she wasn't satisfied with her findings. Her face was now frowned up.

"What the fuck? This shit is drier than a fucking Popeyes biscuit."

I would've laughed if Tanya wasn't so damn serious. She could get a little crazy at times and the last thing I wanted her to think is that I wanted her to get to that level.

Out of nowhere, she attempted to stick two fingers in my vaginal entrance. As much as I didn't want to, I winced in pain. Right now, it was too much for me to handle.

"Like I thought! This shit is swollen as fuck, and it's dry as hell. I'm not dumb! You been giving my pussy up, bitch?"

Shaking my head "no" I yelled, "No, baby. I would never do that. I've been using some toys that I recently got from Spencer's."

I could talk a lot of shit, but right now, I was nervous.

"Okay, show me these new damn toys that you got from Spencer's."

It was as if my body had frozen and I had been consumed with fear. She led me to the bedroom. I didn't know what to do because I knew I hadn't purchased any toys from Spencer's. I even threw out the collection I had with her since I had started messing with Draco right after.

"Tanya, I put those toys in a storage last week," I quickly lied. I didn't realize how silly the lie sounded until it came out of mouth.

I knew Tanya didn't believe me, hell I didn't believe that I had told such a poor life. An evil smile spread across her face.

"Keep digging that hole. It's going to be hard to get out of it."
She pushed me back onto the bed and ripped my shorts off instantly.

"No, Tanya. Please don't," I cried.

"Don't do what? Take what's rightfully mine, even though you've been freely giving it away."

She used her free hand to spread my legs apart. Using her tongue, she forcefully found her way inside.

"Yuck!" She spat on my face, literally. "This pussy doesn't even taste the same no more."

Then get off me delusional ass bitch. I screamed inside of my head.

"Please leave me alone, Tanya," I begged.

"I can't do that. The last time I left you alone, I thought you were working on your nasty ass attitude. Come to find out, ya' ass was fucking around."

Suddenly, she stuck a few fingers inside of me. On top of her being rough as hell, I was also dry as hell. Tears streamed down my face as she roughly fucked me using her fingers. I tried to get out of her grasp, but she was much stronger than me.

"You bitches really are for everybody," she shouted as continued to torture me. I could feel the inside of me burning as she purposely scratched me down there.

Using all the strength I had, I finally was able to free my hands. I smacked the shit out of Tanya. "Get the fuck out before I call the cops and press charges against your ass."

I grabbed the lamp that was on the bedside table and aimed it at Tanya's head. Unfortunately, I missed. I heard my front door slam, which meant that she had left. I called the first person that was in my call log, Draco. He answered on the first ring. It was noisy as hell in the background.

"What's up, bae?"

"Draco. I just got raped," I cried real ugly tears.

"Aye everybody, shut the fuck up," he ordered and sure enough, everyone in the background got quiet as hell. "Yo, run that the fuck back. You said what?"

"I got raped," I repeated, this time crying even more ugly tears. I couldn't believe what I was saying.

"Somebody fucking dying tonight. Where you at?"
"I'm at home."
"Stay on the line. I'm on my way now," he shouted.

Even though the situation was fucked up, I felt much better knowing that I had Draco by my side.

***

CHAPTER FOURTEEN:
DEMARIO SANDERS

Later That Night

We were sitting outside one of Dollar 's trap houses. It was one with less traffic. Even still, we were a few cars deep with 4 occupants in each ride. We had to be ready for whatever when it came to Dollar 's crew. Though the traphouse looked small on the inside, for all we know it could've been twenty mothafuckas in there. We truly didn't know. That's why it was better to be over-prepared than under-prepared.

Tony passed me the blunt. "Just think man, if we successfully hit up one of his trap houses, we can hit up the remaining two. If we successfully do that and get away, it will that Dollar and his crew are weak after all. You will be the first nigga to every trick him out his spot."

Hearing Tony say that had me pumped all the way up. In this moment, I no longer wanted to hit his small trap. I wanted to hit the big trap first and go back to the smaller ones. I had prepared for this moment for years and now I finally had the opportunity considering that I formed my own lil' crew. They were with it too because they knew they would be eating shortly. All we had to do is get rid of Dollar, then his crew would crumble. Then a new nigga would have to step up and I already said that it would be me.

"This traphouse gon' be too damn easy for us. I could probably hit this one up by my damn self. We need to aim bigger," I told Tony and the rest of my partners who were in the backseat.

"Shit, I'm with it if you with it," Shawn said from the backseat. Hearing him say that was like music to my ears. My dick had hardened. It was nothing like a mothafucka who was dumb enough to follow and carry out your orders. Even with the small power I now had, I felt like Dollar. I could only imagine what it would be like once I finally took his throne.

"Let's reroute then. You know I'm down for the cause. Just know we better be clutchin' the trigger at all times cause I'm sure it's a lot of goons in that particular trap house. I'll send out a group message right now."

While Tony sent out the message, we discreetly left one trap house and traveled to the other. I didn't see any cars out that looked like it belonged to Dollar 's crew but I knew better. We parked a few feet down from the trap house. All car lights were shut off. Prior to coming over, I made sure that every occupant ducked in the car until further notice. That way, we wouldn't look suspect. Luckily, there were lots of cars parked on each side of the street.

My stomach started bubbling. A nigga was getting scared. Even though I was surrounded by protection, sitting outside in the pitch dark was creepy as hell. I don't see how Dollar and his crew could come out into the unknown but then again, they probably weren't scared. Niggas probably didn't step on their turf, but I would definitely be the first one today.

"I think I just saw a door open," I said excitedly. There was a little bit of light coming from inside the traphouse.

"I did too," Tony agreed with me. "I'm about to tell these niggas to get ready."

I said a silent prayer. "Y'all ready to run up?"

"Yeah! Don't you niggas get done up out here," Tony joked.

We expeditiously hopped out the car. "As soon as those niggas come out, y'all better be ready to get to bussin'," I commanded. The door opened again. Niggas after niggas were filing out. Some had duffle bags while others had pushcarts loaded down with drugs. I would've been fascinated had this not been a serious moment. Cowering behind somebody's car, I dropped to the ground and started spraying at niggas' legs.

"Y'all picked the wrong niggas," I heard somebody shout from Dollar 's crew.

The voices and shots were getting closer.

POP!

POP!

I heard both crews busting back at each other. It was every man for himself. I quickly slid under the car, not giving a fuck about anybody else. Several footsteps ran past me.

TAT!

TAT!

TAT!

The sound of an AK-47 sounded throughout the neighborhood. I already knew those guns belonged to somebody from Dollar 's crew because we only brought pistols thinking that is what they would've been toting too. Nobody was thinking about military-style weapons. Not us at least. In that moment I realized we hadn't properly planned. I could hear bodies dropping behind me.

I silently prayed that it wasn't any of my niggas. Seeing that the coast was clear because the shots had grown distant, I crawled from underneath the car and into the thick bushes. The door to the trap was left wide open. Judging by the number of footsteps I heard a few seconds ago, I figured that all Dollar 's soldiers had cleared out. It was time for me to make a move and go get at least one bag. It could be some work or a bag of money, either one would've put more money in my pockets.

Quietly, I tiptoed to the entrance. You would've thought I belonged there with the way I walked in. I kept my eyes on the door at the back of the house because I knew more than likely that's where everything was. The traphouse was awfully silent too. I couldn't believe this shit was so damn easy. I managed to not get shot and I was about to steal a bag or two, depending on how I was feeling when I actually got in the room.

This is finna be a lil quick in and out. I thought to myself. I could've hit a Birdman hand rub if I wasn't on a set time. I knew his crew would be coming back sooner or later. A nigga was about to shoot down the hallway until I felt a cold piece of metal pointed in the back of my head. I can't lie, a nigga was shaken.

"I just wanna know where yo' ass think you're going," A female voice said behind me, pressing the gun further into my head. At any second, I felt like I a bullet was about to tear through a nigga's head. I slowly reached for my burner.

BOOM!

The loaded gun had hit the floor with a thud. Now there was a gun to my temple. I already knew who the person was without having to take a look. It was Dollar and it only made sense for the woman's voice behind me to be Keke pretty ass. It was as if shorty had bossed up overnight. She went from "How May I Take Your Order" to straight up serving niggas, literally. Dollar had turned her ass back into a monster.

"What possessed you and yo' niggas to come to my side of town and fuck with a nigga, huh?" Dollar asked me.

Not wanting to seem weak and scared like I really was, I put some extra base in my voice. "Nigga, I was coming to knock you right off your square."

Dollar chuckled. "You don't believe that yourself, do you? You're pussy, lil' nigga. I can smell the fear on you. My girl and me were waiting on a nigga to be stupid and run up in here. We knew the door was open. I've been in this game for years now. Niggas can plot all day and night, but I bet you niggas won't prosper."

Keke finally dropped the gun and we came face to face with each other.

"Demario, I know your ass didn't try to rob nobody," she started laughing like the shit was funny.

Dollar looked from me to Keke. "Say, you know this nigga?"

"Of course, I know Demario. He is the guy that lives in my complex, remember? The one you had a few words with."

"Aw yeah! He does look familiar now that you say that. Bring me a chair and a rope. They're in the hallway closet," he instructed her. Like a little puppet, she scurried off to get it.

She brought the rope and chair.

"What do you want me to do next?" She asked, confirming that she was a puppet like I thought. Bitches would do anything to be considered a nigga's ride or die. She wasn't about that life like the streets loved to claim just like I wasn't.

"Bonnie would have never asked Clyde what she should do next."

"Well this is not Bonnie and Clyde's story, this is ours. Do you want me to tie him up or nah?" I could hear the arrogant sass in her voice.

"Duh, Keke! You've been doing well lately. Don't start fucking up just because you know this cat. Remember, he would've killed us not too long ago."

"Just like they did the real Bonnie and Clyde, huh?" I chuckled despite the unfortunate position I was in. Keke pushed me into the chair and started tying me up while Dollar forced the gun into my mouth.

"Keep talking that tough shit. I'll blow yo' damn tonsils out," Dollar spat.

Just then, his crew came running back in. "We got all those niggas," they cheered.

"All except for this one," Dollar said, pointing at me.

Hearing that none of my niggas made it had me like fuck life. How could I run an empire with no niggas? My vision had died right along with my niggas, especially Tony. I thought about how he was so eager to ride for a nigga and I left him stranded the first chance I got.

"Say, Keke and I are about to get out of here. Take care of that for me."

"Fasho, boss!" The fat nigga said. I could see the hunger in his eyes.

"Anything else you want to say to me before I go?" Dollar asked me.

I figured I was going to die anyway. So why not fuck up Dollar and Keke's relationship.

"Nah, I got something to say to Keke, though."

She spun around on her heels with a frown on her face. "What do you have to say to me?"

"Dollar fucked Misha a few nights ago. He --," I started to run off at the mouth but the cold feeling of the gun to my temple made me stop myself. Keke moved Dollar 's hand out the way.

"Nah, finish what you were about to say," Keke commanded.

"Like I said, he pulled up to her place a few nights ago. I saw him because I was outside. I even spoke to the nigga."

"Oh, that was you?" Dollar asked. He closed his mouth just as quickly when Keke gave him that look. He knew he had confirmed what I was saying all along.

"Street rule #1, you don't fuck snitch!" Keke barked. She took the gun and brought it across my face. I could hear my teeth breaking instantly.

"Let's fucking go, Dollar," She seethed.

As soon as they walked out the door, he started walking up on me. I already knew what time it was then. It was lights out for a nigga...

***

CHAPTER FOURTEEN:
MISHA SIMS
THE TRAP

The Next Day

At any moment now, I was waiting on Dollar to walk through that door after I threatened him with a potential pregnancy. He didn't show up as expected. I called him so much that she eventually powered off her phone. I was going to get his ass home to me one way or another. As much as I didn't want to, I see that it was time to put this piece of paper to use.

I went inside of my bedroom and grabbed the paper that I stuffed under my mattress just in case he came over. It had Dollar 's license plate number on it that I kept for my own convenience. After Googling New Orleans's police department non-emergency number, I called them up. Someone picked up after a few rings.

"Hi, ma'am. Who can I speak with about reporting possible drug-related activity?" I asked the woman on the other end of the phone.

"You're speaking to the right person, ma'am! You can report the information to me, and I can pass it along," The clerk informed me.

"I have reasonable suspicion to believe that my child's father is distributing drugs all over again. He was recently released from the pen not even a good month ago, but I think he has gone back to his old lifestyle."

"Ma'am, what's your child's father name and do you have any extra information such as a description of his or her car. Maybe you even have a license plate number or something that would make the suspect easily recognizable."

"Yes ma'am, I have all of that for you." I gave her all of Dollar 's information. I recited the year, make and model of his car. Hell, I didn't know much about Keke, but I told the dispatch that she would possibly be an accomplice.

"Thank you, ma'am. I will surely pass this on. If they find something, someone will contact you."

That was all I needed to know. To take it a step further, I went online and found the Drugs Enforcement Agency and the Department of Justice's contact numbers. If I didn't hear anything back from New Orleans police within a week, I damn sure was going to pass this information along to NOPD AGAIN.

In my eyes, I wasn't doing anything wrong. All Dollar had to do is follow my rules and compensate me through love for the way I held him down when he was locked up. The same trouble he was about to find himself back in, I tried my hardest to keep him out of. I even came up with a plan for him to invest his drug money and turn them into lucrative businesses, but he obviously didn't want that. He had been on his high horse long enough. Now it was time to bring his ass down...

***

CHAPTER SIXTEEN:
KEKE JONES
MY MAMA WAS RIGHT

Later That Night

Everything in my life had started moving so fast around Dollar now that we were official again. I knew I was no longer the reformed girl who walked inside the club the night of the big celebration.

It was late at night; Dollar and I were headed to his traphouse to deliver the drugs I begged him to bring back to his house so that we could break it down and bag it up together. I went from operating a store outside of my apartment to making constant trips to the traphouse.

I had gotten lost in my thoughts while Dollar drove. I couldn't believe I had pistol whipped a nigga last night. Shit, I really couldn't believe half of the things I had done within this this month – from fucking with my soulmate again to dealing with drugs again to messing with a gun for the first time ever. My life was high-key lit. It was so lit that I hadn't actually talked to my best friend in a few days. I figured I would give Dollar and me a day apart so that I could go visit her. Just as I was about to tell Dollar that I would be visiting Jazzy tomorrow, a pair of blue lights began flashing behind us.

"What the fuck does these niggas want?" Dollar said aloud. "Just relax! Start stuffing some of that work inside your clothes and bags.

More than likely, it will be a cop that's been informed of the relationship we all have. Just put that shit up for just in case purposes.

Without asking any questions, I quickly began stuffing the drugs underneath my oversized cardigan. It was a good thing that I had brought it since Dollar loved to keep the air blasting in his rides. As soon as I finished stuffing the last bag inside of me, the cop walked over to Dollar 's window. He rolled the window down while I did mental yoga to ease my mind and play normal.

"Good afternoon, sir," The white, fat officer greeted Dollar.
"Sup," Dollar responded dryly. I knew he couldn't have been one of the cops on his payroll just by the way he responded.

"It's sure late as hell. Where are y'all going?" The officer asked while particularly shining his light on me. "Is she pregnant?"

"Yeah, she is," Dollar responded abruptly, which I'm glad he did because a lump formed in my throat as I thought about the time the FEDS raided our spot.

He chuckled; well it was a rather fake one. "Oh, is that right? Do you know how far along is she?"

Now agitated, Dollar asked, "Does it fucking matter? What is your reason for stopping me? I'm going 5 miles under the speed limit not over it!"

"Actually sir, I'm not stopping you. I'm stopping her."

My body tensed up. That's when I looked out my mirror and noticed another officer walking up to my side of the car.

"We received a tip that the young lady has been distributing drugs and she is considered to be armed and dangerous as well."

"That's a got damn lie! She's innocent as hell. Y'all mothafuckas don't even know her," Dollar spat. I could tell he was getting heated at this very moment. I wanted to calm him down, but a bitch was in the hot seat my damn self.

"Her name is Keke Jones and we received a tip not too long ago. If she's innocent like you say she is, then the other officer can prove that right here, right now. So, let's settle this once and for all."

The second officer knocked on the window while telling me to roll my window down.

"Do you have some identification on you, ma'am?"

Trying to appear normal, I flashed a huge, quaky smile. "No sir, I don't. I left it at home since I'm not driving."

"Okay, but you're always supposed to have some form of I.D. on you, no matter who is driving. That is some round, smelly ass belly you have there," he called me out. "Do you mind stepping out the car for me?"

By now, I was sweating as if I had popped too many damn mollies. Even with the air on full-blast, I was now hot as hell.

"Dollar, what do I do next?" I whispered with a shaky voice, reliving that terrible day all over again.

Out of the corner of my eye, I could see him shaking his head. "Just do as they say, baby. Fuckkkkk!"

Not really wanting to, I finally stepped out the car. The bricks I had stuffed in my cardigan hit the cement with no shame at all.

All I could hear was my mom's voice in my ear telling me that I had completely fucked up! Damn!

***

TO BE CONTINUED…